Four Seasons of

Ecstasy...

A Novel

By Mahogany Star

Acknowledgements

Thank you God for allowing me to express my thoughts through writing, and thank you for blessing me each day in so many ways. I'm thankful for those who came before me, for my grandmother and her mother and my ancestors that prayed for me before I got here. To my husband, Michael, thank you for loving me on my worst days, thank you for your patience. Thank you for being such a great father, you would think I made you up in a story...LOL. You're a dream, I love you. We've grown together and I'm forever grateful for each day with you. My children Michael-Jalen and Madison, I love you both with my whole entire everything. I hope my love is something you will keep with you forever in your hearts and minds. To my mama, Max I love you so much, I hope I tell you that enough.

To my sister Monique and my niece Mikaylah, I love you both. Thank you for extending my family circle. My aunt Tai, I love you and I'm so blessed to have an aunt who's so dear to my heart, I'm so fond of you! I think you know that though. To my Rozier, Colon, Martin and Porter families, I'm blessed with the loving circle you have formed around me. Lu and Ni, love you I couldn't imagine my childhood without you. Sadri, my oldest friend, and my sis I love you. Nagina, thank you for being my big sis, a supporter and advocate of my work! Thank you for helping me name this follow-up to Summer's Heat. Kandece, thank you for always providing feedback no matter how many times I ask. Twanna, Tammy love you both, thank you for your friendship and support. Bebe, thank you for always supporting me and pushing me even when I drag my feet. Thank you for really believing in my talent. Ricky, I'm proud of you. That children's book is so awesome! Thank you Teairrah Reid for your editing work. Thank you to the team at Sexxtacular for having me on my first podcast. I know I'm forgetting people but I wanted to keep this short. I can't forget to thank those who read my stories! I'm so grateful.

-

Mahogany

People come into your life for a reason, a season, or a lifetime. -
Author Unknown

Previously in Summer's Heat...

I rushed through the airport going through the check-in process quicker than I expected. I got to the terminal and sat down and breathed a sigh of relief. Having the garage's service pick me up had been a life saver. After leaving Dre's apartment I rushed back to the hotel jumped in the shower and finished my last minute packing in a flash.

I knew Dre was probably just turning over and wondering where I had disappeared to. I looked at my cellphone and decided that it was my last connection to what I knew. I looked at the random faces of people who some like me were trying to get away for whatever reason. I searched until I found a little bar like restaurant so that I could take a few shots of the clear juice before boarding, I figured on an empty stomach I would absorb the alcohol more quickly.

I saw a small bar with neon blue lighting welcoming me and walked in.

The bar was fairly empty with only a few other patrons there for service, most of them looked like business men passing through. Usually they would be easy marks, I'd make eye contact slide them my business card and wait for the call.

Not today.

"Traveling alone?" The grey haired bartender with a heavy Latin accent asked as I sat down and he placed a cocktail menu in front of me.

"Yes." I kept it short. I wasn't in the mood for the small talk. I just wanted my drink and quick.

"I'll take three shots of patron. Patron Lime." I asked.

"Three at one time?" He asked like he hadn't heard me the first time.

"How about one after the other. So every time I finish one you put another down." I looked at him with a raised eyebrow and said.

I took my shots down quickly. One after the other, the liquid settling and burning my stomach a bit. It didn't take long for me to feel the effect. I suddenly felt a little lighter on my feet, optimistic about what lie ahead on the sunny west coast.

"Maybe it'll be Vegas, then Los Angeles, or maybe I should go to Miami for a little while." I thought to myself.

I looked at the time on the wall and noticed it was getting close to boarding time. I paid for my shots and wandered back over to the terminal

As I made my way over to the seating area at the boarding area I saw a group of women who looked to be in their late twenties to early thirties and I wondered if they had it figured out yet. They were engrossed in conversation laughing hysterically. I wondered and speculated on what they could be laughing about so early in the morning. One of the women, an attractive caramel colored woman with a funky short haircut looked at me and smiled, I guess she caught my observation.

My phone's ringing broke our eye time and I looked down to see Dre's face across my screen. I rejected the call, turned the phone off and looked around until I spotted the nearest trash can. I picked up my carryon that housed my laptop and important documents and searched for a few napkins. I found the napkins and wrapped as many as I could around my cellphone before tossing it in the trash. I didn't want people to notice that it was a cellphone that was being tossed so I tried to disguise it in tissue.

The announcement came over the speakers that it was time to board the Jet Blue nonstop flight bound for Las Vegas. I made my way to the line eager to get on board and relax. I stood in line behind the group of women trying not to ease drop.

I heard the light skin thick one speak with a heavy southern accent, "I told him we were stopping in New York and then making our way to Vegas for the remainder of our trip. All he knows is I come home happy and that's all he cares about." She said as the pretty tall dark skin lady with long silky bra strap length hair and who happened to have on the most fabulous Gucci shades says as she tips her shades over her nose and looks at her friend "and that's all he needs to know." She wasn't laughing when she spoke at all. I liked her style already.

I put my carryon in the overhead compartment and took my seat by the window. It felt good to settle into my seat and relax. I wanted to take a nice long nap so that I could be refreshed when I landed but before I dozed I opened my bag and pulled out my laptop and decided to send Dre an email. I didn't want to hurt him and decided he should know why I left the way I did.

Dre,

You're probably reading this wondering where I am and why I'm not answering your calls. It is probably not something that'll even make sense to you today but maybe one day it will. As it stands today Dre, I love you more than I love any physical thing in this world outside of myself. But as I have come to learn in this world, love is fleeting, for the moment, not fixed but always changing. Before you, I hadn't ever experience a feeling so warm, so genuine, so real. You're my first true love Dre. The man I've always dreamed of. You think I'm what you've always dreamed of, and perhaps I am right now. But as I have learned there's always conditions to the love between man and woman. I love you today because of the high you have me on today. That may not be tomorrow. I refuse to ever trust anyone with my heart. I won't become someone's temporary satisfaction. The one thing I've learned in my young life Dre is that everything and I do mean everything is temporary. With that lesson I've decided to keep it moving physically and emotionally. Unfortunately, I learned this lesson early in life, and vowed from to never let anyone have the power to discard me or my feelings. I've experienced how you can be loved so much in one moment and in the next be tossed aside like yesterday's trash. As much as I love you, I can't give you or anyone else that power either. I hope in time you find what you need, whoever that may be. You have a lot to offer a woman Dre, the woman that believes in marriage, kids, and a white picket fence. That woman is not me.

I love you Dre, I probably always will, but sometimes love ain't enough.

Forever, Summer

Prologue

Summer

One thing is for certain, and two things are for sure; nothing stays the same. Not love, life, situations, relationships, and certainly not the worst of times. Two years ago, I was unsure about everything. I was selling my ass and the ass of others to cover the cost of the lifestyle I refused to let go. I dropped out of school one semester shy of graduating with a dual Bachelor's-Master's Degree in Business Administration. I was doubtful about love, life, my future. I left everything including the love of my life behind, all without a plan. I just knew I needed to get away from New York and all the drama that it held for me. I never imagined that a chance encounter with three women would turn my world around.

I met Wynter, Spree, and Fallon on a flight to Las Vegas. When the flight landed, we made small talk as we waited for our luggage, but the connection was nearly instantaneous. Wynter, who was the best big sister to us all, was what I aspired to be. She was beautiful, smart, and from a broken home. She said the look in my eyes reminded her of her own. Wynter was an Attorney and she owned her own law firm. Before that, she was a stripper who said she was stripping to pay for school, only she was serious. At five-nine with rich chocolate skin and brown eyes, she was thick in all the places men liked. Like me, she learned early on that men were only as loyal as their options. When her parents moved her and her brother to Atlanta in the height what has now become Blacklanta, she never thought that would be the end of everything normal. They moved into a big place, a mini mansion compared to the home they had in Cary, North Carolina, when her dad's position at the pharmaceutical company was promoted and relocated. But her mom apparently was no match for the small waists, big asses, aggressive charm of the southern bells that welcomed her father with open arms and open legs. Six months into their move, her father had taken up with some woman and had started playing daddy to her kids. By the time Wynter was sixteen, she had been initiated illegally into the nightlife that had been helpful in helping her mother pay the bills when her father decided his new home and his new family came first. What Wynter got from this is to never ever depend on a man to pay your bills or trust a man with your heart. It gave her a no-nonsense work ethic. She was serious about all things financial. Her appearance was impeccable as she exercised religiously. She loved sex, but for her, that came easy. Wynter kept a lover or two on rotation, but when they got too serious, she cut them the fuck off.

Spree met Wynter five years ago when she needed representation during her divorce. Spree's husband, her high-school sweetheart, was a successful R&B producer, who had a few women kept, like most men in the industry. Only Spree, unlike other wives, was not one to stick around when her husband of five years decided to come home and tell her that his side chick was expecting. This was especially painful to Spree as she gone through several rounds of fertility treatments with no success. She hired Wynter to represent her, and not only did she become her lawyer, but she became family. Wynter saw her own mother's pain written all over Spree. Wynter obtained a nice settlement from the divorce for Spree and helped her make her life over, starting with a head-to-toe makeover. Wynter wasn't the biggest fan of quick fixes, but she knew Spree was suffering from self-esteem issues after years of being compared to the video vixens her husband was bedding, and as a result, feeling less than. She set her up with an appointment at the well-known Miami plastic surgeon's office. With fat transfers, D-cup implants, and the slightest injections of fillers, Spree went from the shy, soft-spoken woman, to the Coca Cola bottle-shaped, big ass, big titty, irresistible, butter-pecan eye candy any man would want a taste of. They made it a girl's trip, in which she included her best friend of almost twenty years, Fallon. While they spent almost a month in Miami during her recovery, Spree was introduced into a new body and new a lifestyle, which included dick and more dick. It was an exhilarating sense of freedom and control, something that Spree was not familiar with but was more than willing to get used to.

Fallon was successful in her own right. She had created a line of organic skin-care products in her kitchen right out of high school. She started off selling face and body butters to friends and family, but when her aunt encouraged her to start vending at trade shows, her business began to take off. Fallon had no idea when she became a parent at the tender age of fourteen how she was going to make it, but with her mother's help, she raised a daughter, who was away at school, enjoying her second year of college. Her daughter's father, a senior and the star of their high school football team, had big dreams of going to the NFL, but his dreams did not include being tied down with a wife and baby at a young age. So his parents made sure he went off to college, and eventually, he was picked up by a team on the West Coast. Bryan didn't do much in terms of the day-to-day parenting. On occasion, he'd send for Brianna whenever his new wife thought it was politically correct for Brianna to be in their pictures. But for the most part, Fallon's mother parented Brianna, even more than Fallon. Fallon was grateful for this help, and while she didn't go to college, she had made quite the life for herself. Five years ago, her skin-care line went national, and over the past year, it had gone international. Fallon was what some men deemed "exotic" in her looks. Her parents emigrated from Guyana just before she was born. So while her mother was still a practicing Hindu-Indian, she and her father adapted to the southern culture, with her father opting for biscuits instead of their traditional roti.

She had been serious a few years prior with a man she'd met during the course of business. He was an author who wrote self-help books for men on relationships, and he had a syndicated radio show. He was indeed romantic, a poet even. He treated Fallon like a queen, serenading her with poetic words about her beauty, putting her name in ink, naming one the chapters in what became a bestselling book after her. He took her on trips, bought her expensive gifts, and introduced her products to celebrities who may not have otherwise known of her skin-care line. It was a good deal, a great relationship, and as a bonus, he also happened to be great in bed. The problem was that he was still romanticizing every woman that he came across. Turns out he was bedding actresses he met during interviews, his publicist, and whomever else he could manage to get his dick in. After that relationship, Fallon realized that Wynter was onto something when it came to her theory about men and love. Wynter rationalized men as being nothing more than non-monogamous creatures.

"They don't have the ability to be monogamous. Their brains are wired so that once they've had a few dips inside your pool, their interest in you is over. That moment of feigned interest has come and gone, and now they want to see how deep the next river is," Wynter would say.

Wynter's theory had been proven time and time again through the experiences of women all over the world. Wynter advised any woman within earshot, "If you can have, raise, and support your kids on your own, do it. If you don't want kids, don't have them. Live by the rules you create. Have sex. Fuck who you want, when you want, but have enough sense to protect yourself and value your health, but shit, at the end of the day, do you!"

The Forecast

Summer sat in the exclusive restaurant in the heart of Atlanta waiting for her family of friends to arrive. She picked up the complimentary glass of wine and smiled. Wynter had planned this celebratory dinner in Summer's honor. Just two years ago, Summer was a college dropout, but with Wynter and the other's guidance, Summer re-enrolled in school and completed her dual bachelor's-master's degree. Summer was now the owner of one of the hottest celebrity blogs on social media. She had amassed a huge following and seemed to be the first with all the juicy entertainment gossip that kept her followers coming back for more. When they met in Las Vegas, Spree invited Summer to lunch with the ladies, and they'd been thick as thieves ever since.

Summer thought she'd be in Vegas for a while, but at Wynter's invitation to stay with her, she decided she would see what Atlanta had to offer. Just as she picked up her phone to group text her friends to ask them why they were late, she saw them entering the restaurant, looking like Charlie's angels. They had the attention of everyone as they walked in looking like they were walking down a runway. Fallon carried a beautiful bouquet of white roses, Wynter carried a large gift box from Gucci, and Spree a large shopping bag from Givenchy.

Summer, who wasn't quick to cry, couldn't help but tear up at the sight. She had grown to love the ladies very much in a short time.

Wynter treated Summer like the daughter and sister she never had. She was very protective over Summer, and like Wynter, Spree and Fallon adored her as well.

"I thought you bitches would never get here!" Summer said through tears and laughter as she stood up to group hug her friends.

"Chick, if you don't take these damn flowers out of my hands," Fallon teased, nearly tearing herself.

They knew Summer had been through a lot and had seen a lot in her short years. The group formed a tight circle around Summer as the newest and youngest sister in the group. They thought it was important to always make her feel loved.

After dinner, they got into the small talk about what was going on in their lives. Wynter looked at the ladies and smirked sneakily while sipping her champagne.

"I know that look. What are you up to?" Spree asked.

"I'm not up to a damn thing. That's the problem. Y'all know the pickings is slim here in the A," Wynter said as she looked around the table.

"Who you telling? Pickings get any slimmer, I might have to start eating pussy," Fallon mumbled.

"I don't know how y'all did it down here all these years. Even the broke men down here get to fuck and juggle a few chicks at a time. I ain't never seen no shit like this. Dudes with no ends getting so much ass," Summer said as she sucked her teeth.

Wynter leaned forward before speaking. "Any of you getting fucked like you wanna right now?"

"Tori's been doing his thing," Summer offered, mentioning the attorney she had recently began dating.

"Well, I've hit a dry patch, and my cootie don't like to be dry," Spree said.

They all chuckled, but Wynter took that as her opportunity to lecture.

"Doesn't sound like any of us are getting the dick we deserve."

"I'll second that!" Fallon said, raising her champagne glass.

"Well, I'm not complaining about Tori. He's no Dre, but again, I'm not complaining," Summer stated.

"This ain't about complaining. This is about celebrating. I don't hear you celebrating that dick either," Wynter said as she rolled her eyes.

"I mean, it's definitely good. I could teach him a few new tricks. I'm molding that dick into what I want it to be," Summer said as she sipped her champagne.

She could feel the eyes of her best friends on her. She knew they were about to go in.

"Mold him? Mold the dick? I don't got time to be teaching no grown ass man how to make my kitty wet. If he ain't offering that heroine dick, throw that fish back in the ocean."

"Heroine dick?" Summer asked, her eyes wide.

Fallon took this as her opportunity to interject.

"Um, yeah. There's levels to this shit. You got the weed dick, crack dick, coka dick, heroine dick, and ether. Now with weed being the lowest grade of a high you get on this drug chart, imagine as it relates to the D. I, myself, really enjoy the heroine, better knowns as HD. Coka is even acceptable, but girl, if you ever get that ether! You'll be circling his house in the daylight looking for your next hit!" Fallon gestured like she had a flashlight in her hand.

The ladies all bust out in laughter so loud that a few of the patrons at other tables looked over in disgust.

"I say we all go out and find that quality HD! If you can score ether, well then that's a major plus! But don't come back to our next dinner looking all strung the fuck out." Wynter managed to say through laughter.

Wynter was probably the most serious one out of the group and especially serious when it came to sex. So they all relished in watching her laugh and let her hair down for a bit.

Wynter

"Every season is one of becoming, but not always one of

blooming. Be gracious with your ever-evolving self." -B. Oakman

*I raised my hands in front of my face, but I couldn't even see
them. Complete and total darkness as far as my eyes can stretch. Yet
my skin felt like the finest of hairs are standing up. I felt fingertips...
No, maybe it's a feather as it glides up my arm, over my shoulder,
and down to my breasts ever so lightly. My nipples protruded—hard,
tender, and so sensitive that the light brush across them sent a
pulsating shot straight to my clitoris. Wait. My legs were parted, and
a moist tongue glided up my right leg. I was already slightly shaking.
Then it was there... the pulsating pressure... the heat from his breath
at my opening. I heard him panting. His breath was warm and heavy
as he sucked on my clit. I ground my pelvis into his face as I held the
back of his head. Oh, you're about to get all of this. My body jerked
as I exploded, but he didn't let me savor the peak I'd just reached.
He filled me up entirely and began thrusting. I couldn't catch my
breath. I wrapped my hands around his broad shoulders as he lifted
me up and wrapped my legs around his waist, not missing a beat
with his strokes. It was still dark. I reached out for something that
would make him familiar. I rubbed my hands over his head; it's
bald. I caressed his face as he stuck his delicious tongue in my
mouth. Yummy! It tasted like mint and me. Goatee. Light five o'clock*

shadow. He moved faster. His hands were soft as they gripped my ass and held me firm and steady. He went as deep as my body allowed, and then I felt his dick throb.

The sun peeked through my custom-made wooden blinds, causing me to wake up just before my mystery man gave me my second orgasm. I rolled over and watched the smooth ripples that displayed thick muscles in his almond-colored back as he pulled his T-shirt over his head. We had a few rounds of sex last night, but he was not the one causing my body to spasm in my dream. I knew his touch, and the man in my dream was unfamiliar.

He had long since stopped protesting having to leave at the crack of dawn every time I allowed him to stay over. Vic was lucky enough to get to spend a few post-coital hours napping in my bed, but I was nice to him since he was very good at pleasing me. It had always been a rule of mine to never ever let a man get comfortable at my place. That means, not nary sock, toothbrush, durag, tie, underwear, not even a stray hair is to be left at my place. Important words here: *My Place*. I worked too hard for any man to come in thinking my shit belonged to him, in any way, shape, or form. Fuck outta here.

Most of the time, I didn't bring them to my place, but I had been dealing with Vic for almost a year, seeing him when I felt I needed a good release. Vic was gorgeous by any woman's standards. Body of an African warrior with bone structure and slanted eyes much like the model Tyson Beckford, Vic was used to having his way with the ladies. Only thing is, he had met his match in me. I actually liked Vic enough. He was in construction, and manual labor had given him the rough hands that felt good and rough against my soft skin. But liking him wasn't enough for me, and while I could tolerate dinner and a nice roll around the sack with him, there couldn't and wouldn't be much more. Baby mamas was something I had no intention of doing, and Vic had two. One was one too many, so there was no way I was going to get seriously involved with a dude that had two.

Vic grabbed his wallet off the nightstand and knelt to kiss me. As always, I had gotten up at four and brushed my teeth before lying back down. I welcomed his moist lips and slipped him a slither of tongue but ended it promptly. I had no time for round three of his acrobatics.

"Call me, Wyn," he said as he made his way to my bedroom door.

"I always do," I said, waving him away.

Vic paused by my door, shaking his head at me as if he couldn't believe me. I couldn't help but wonder if I would ever desire any man's company for longer than twenty-four hours. But as quickly as that thought came, it disappeared as I thought about the busy day I had ahead of me at my office. Grateful that I had a caseload that's filled to the brim and a business partner who's as trustworthy and diligent as I have in Greg, I shake off the idea of love when it comes to mind, and that's not too often. Representing many women and men in matters of the heart and finance has really been an eye-opening experience. Not that it's any surprise, but I know people hurt each other all the time, but the levels people go to, to hide not only their lovers, but to hide their money! You'd be surprised at the amount of secret accounts people are holding on to, never trusting anyone enough to fully divulge, always keeping a "break in case of emergency" stash. So what's the point? It's certainly not for me to figure out since I don't see myself ever having to deal with this shit. I sat on the side of my bed, pausing to think about the day ahead.

I walked into my office, pausing briefly by the large bronze and gold plaque that read: Williams & Mathis Attorneys at Law. No matter how many times I walk past these doors, I never get over the fact that I did it. This my firm! I employ people. I'm an attorney, and a damn good one at that! Sheila looked away from her screen to say good morning. I know she was probably on some gossip site and not really working, but it doesn't bother me because she gets her job done.

"Good morning, Wynter. The coffee's almost finished brewing. I'll bring your cup right in." She spews.

"Thanks, Sheila. I need it damn near black. I had a long night," I mumbled as I made my way to my office.

I could feel Sheila on my tail rambling on about this or that.

"Don't forget you leave for New York tomorrow for the National Annual Attorneys Seminar."

"Tomorrow? Is it that time already?"

"Yes. I printed your itinerary. It's on your desk along with all of your hotel information. Tomorrow night is the mixer. Should be fun." Sheila gushed.

"It's hardly ever fun. Just a bunch of stuffy men and a few women all trying to act like they're smarter than each other. Shit, I wish I hadn't told you to book me this year." I huffed.

I love New York, but I liked to be in the mindset to travel, and I hadn't even thought about what I would be taking with me. I sat down at my desk and went through my emails. I wasn't going to spend a lot of time at the office today. I needed to get home and pack for cold ass New York. Ughh.

I opened my suitcase and pulled out a casual yet expensive pantsuit for tonight's mixer. It was in one of the ballrooms of an elaborate Times Square hotel that they held the conference in. I got in early this morning, and after settling in, I did a little shopping in some of my favorite stores on Fifth Avenue. You just didn't get this type of luxury in Atlanta. After showering and getting dressed, I made my way down to the hotel ballroom prepared for a night of shallow conversation and observation of ostentatious behavior.

I made my way over to the open bar and ordered a cocktail. "Seltzer, cranberry, and vodka please."

"Oh, a woman who shares my taste in libations. Very nice," I heard the deep baritone voice coming in from right behind me. I turned around, and my eyes were pleased. In one quick swipe over from head to toe, I took in this stranger. Tall enough at about six foot two, deep-brown skin, full lips that were embraced by a neat goatee that held a sprinkling of gray hairs, a bald head, and round eyes. His expensive blazer and cufflinks told me that he, too, was here on business before he even introduced himself.

"I would offer to get you a drink, but since you've already done that, I'll take this as an opportunity to introduce myself. I'm Khalil Jameson."

His name was familiar, so I extended my hand to greet him.

"Khalil Jameson? Of Jameson and Patrick?" I asked, pleasantly surprised.

"That would be me. May I have the pleasure of knowing your name?"

It was then that I realized that he was still holding my hand.

"Wynter. Wynter Williams," I said as I released my hand from his hold. His scent caused the little strands of hair on the back of my neck to stand up. I watched him lick his lips. It looked like he was licking them in slow motion before he spoke.

He motioned for the bartender to come over to where we were standing. "I'll have what this beautiful young lady's having."

After receiving his cocktail, he turned his attention back to me. "Wynter Williams? I finally come face-to-face with the impeccable Wynter? Your reputation really does precede itself, you know? I know you're quite dexterous in the courtroom, but I had no idea that your beauty matched your talent."

As dark as my skin is, I think it still turned red from his compliment. I don't know if it was the fact that I was already horny, but his aura and energy was turning me on.

"Is that so? Well, I can appreciate a compliment. Especially when it's coming from someone of your caliber. Jameson and Patrick have quite the reputation themselves." I sipped my cocktail.

"I'm sure you already knew that your reputation was very good. That's why you're here amongst the best. No?" He raised his eyebrow and extended his arm.

"Why don't we find a table and sit so we can enjoy our drinks and this extravagant dinner I hear they have on the menu for us tonight?"

We sat and made small talk while eating butter-soaked lobster and tender filet mignon that tasted like it had been marinating for days. We were laughing so much as we shared stories that I was concerned we would be frowned upon. So we decided to leave the stuffy ass ballroom full of pomp and circumstance. Khalil asked me if I wanted to walk out of the hotel and find a local lounge, and I was totally with it. We ended up at a dimly-lit, little establishment a few blocks from the hotel. As we entered the Manhattan, after-work patrons didn't look up. They were all engrossed in their after-work chatter, letting the stress of the workweek pass between them. Khalil placed his hand on the small of my back and guided me toward a small, candlelit table near the window.

He told me about his successful business law practice in Jacksonville, Florida. Khalil also shared that he was a divorced father of two high-school aged daughters whom he adored. He said that he dated but hadn't been in a serious relationship since his divorce five years ago. I shared that I was single and had no children and that I liked it that way. Khalil laughed at my bluntness.

"You like it that way? Okay. When was the last time you were in a relationship?"

"What do you mean a relationship? I have plenty of friendships, if that's what you're asking."

"No, Wynter. When's the last time you had a man? A man in your life who made sure you were good. A man who wondered if you took time out of your day to eat."

I interrupted him. "I have a secretary who does that."

"A man who brought you soup when you were home under the weather. Or one you can just call and tell about your day."

"Not to be brash, but I have a great set of friends that I can do that with. To tell you the truth, the only thing I need a man for is to fuck. Dick," I said and winked my eye at him. I had every intention of seeing what Mr. Jameson was about in bed before the weekend was over.

"So that's all you need a man for? To give you orgasms?" Khalil smirked.

"Shit, I can even do that on my own, but I do like the touch of a man. So yeah… I guess that's really all I need a man for." I was smug.

Khalil tapped his glass against mine lightly and asked me if I was ready to call it a night. I could've sat there a little longer talking and people watching, but the shift in Khalil's body language told me he had enough of me for the evening.

The walk back to the hotel was quiet. Each of us was lost in our own thoughts. I wanted to invite Khalil to my room so I could see if his sexy outward persona matched what he was serving up in the bedroom. Khalil seemed distracted and unenthused as we made our way back to the hotel. The lively conversation we had on our way to the bar was a drastic contrast to the silence that lingered between us now. What I didn't feel in terms of the cool New York temperature on my way to get drinks, I totally felt now... cold.

Khalil and I rode the elevator up in silence. I was so annoyed by his silence. I couldn't wait to get off and away from him. Here I was having a good time enjoying his company, damn near ready to serve him up my panty pie on a platter, and he gives me his handsome ass to kiss. I had never been so insulted.

As the elevator doors opened, I began to step off when I felt a gentle tug on my arm. "I enjoyed getting to know you a little, Wynter. I'd like to do this again... soon."

I was confused. "You could've fooled me," I responded dryly as I stepped off the elevator without looking back. *Fuck. Outta. Here. Mr. Cavalier!* I thought to myself as I waved my room key in front of my door, thinking about the empty, king-sized bed I had waiting for me.

Just as I was patting the corners of my mouth with my napkin after savoring the delicious spread of eggs and fruit, Khalil took a seat next to me… without asking. I rolled my eyes without thinking about where I was.

"I hope you had a good night's rest," Khalil said as he motioned the waiter to come over with the hot coffee.

"I rested. Could've slept better though." I was sarcastic. *Especially if I had some dick,* I thought.

We sat through the seminar, elbow to elbow, making small talk between presenters. After lunch was served, the conference ended for the day. I was all set to hit the hotel gym, do a little more shopping, and then treat myself to an expensive dinner at one of New York's many fancy restaurants. I made small talk and exchanged a few pleasantries with attorneys from all over the country and was about to make my way out of the ballroom when I smelled the familiar scent.

"Wynter! Where are you off to this evening?" Khalil inquired.

I spun on my heels, determined not to let him see how excited I was that he still seemed a bit interested. "You're asking because? I mean, after last night, I thought you had enough of my company."

"Enough of your company? Oh, Wynter, we're just getting started." Khalil smirked.

"Is that so?" I said, trying my best not to seem too impressed.

"Yes it's so. I'm determined to know you inside and out." He let out a sly chuckle.

"OK, I see you. I don't have any plans etched in stone. I was just going to do a little of this or that."

"Let me take you to dinner. Make it a better night than last night. I promise," Khalil said as he held his hands together like he was praying.

Khalil told me he had made seven o'clock reservations for dinner at Jean-Georges in Midtown. I agreed to dinner and told him that I would meet him in the lobby at six-thirty.

We rode in the town car in silence to the restaurant. Khalil looked so fucking good in a pair of slacks and a crisp white shirt that wasn't buttoned to the top. I sat across from him nibbling on my food thinking about all the things I wanted to do to him. He licked his lips in between bites of his Chilean sea bass. He darted his tongue over his top lip to get a dab of cream that the crème brûlée he had left across his luscious mouth. "You're not hungry? You've been playing with that salmon. Eat, baby. Don't be shy," Khalil teased.

"Oh, I'm hungry. I just have an appetite for something other than what's on my plate." I flirted back, taking a large swallow of my red wine to wet my throat.

"I see." I watched Khalil dab the corners of his mouth before waving the waiter over. He asked for the check and then turned his attention back to me. "Now let's see if I can fill that appetite of yours." He smiled slyly.

I could feel the liquid slowly seep from my opening. I wanted nothing more at the moment than to have this fine specimen of a man fill me up if only for one night. Shit, make my trip to New York worth more than the shopping and the boring conference agenda.

The driver held the door of our town car open, and we quickly made our way in seeking warmth. The chill in the air hit me as soon as the restaurant door opened. I scooted over, and Khalil sat close to me. His body heat was radiating, making me feel warm inside. He placed his hand on my exposed knee and began a slow, light stroke with his index finger, up and down the fleshy part of my thigh. Khalil moved in and kissed me lightly on the lips, and I returned the kiss with a full-on open mouth, devouring of his lips and tongue. Khalil reciprocated and upped me one. Moving his lips to my neck, he placed passionate kisses all over my collarbone as he grabbed my thigh, and his hand made its way under my dress. My nipples hardened against my silky blouse at the feel of his fingertips as he gripped where my thigh met my opening. I was just about to hike my skirt up to give him the access he needed when I felt the car come to a full halt.

I straightened my blouse and smoothed down my skirt as our driver opened the door and helped me out. The brisk air was a welcomed cool down from the heat I was just feeling. We made our way into the hotel and waited for the elevator. Khalil's eyes were low and sexy. He didn't have the same look that he had yesterday or even earlier this evening. The look of desire he was exuding... It was so fucking sexy. I couldn't wait to see if he was able to live up to the look he had in his eyes. We got in the elevator with a few strangers and some other attorneys who we met during the convention. They had been enjoying their time in New York as well. One older attorney had a pretty, young, leggy blonde on his arm, and the other reeked of alcohol. Letting down their stuffy exterior, they didn't look anything like the conservatives they did just that morning at breakfast. Go figure. Khalil and I both nodded pleasantries. The sexual energy in the air was palpable. In the tightness of the packed elevator, Khalil reached for my hand. The simple gesture was just what I needed. I was craving any part of him that I could feel.

When we got to the twenty-fourth floor, the elevator opened, and I excused myself past a few passengers, still holding onto his hand. As soon as we stepped off the elevator, Khalil was behind me, kissing my neck his groin on my ass. His hard dick was sitting right between my ass cheeks. I relished in the feeling of his tongue on my neck, but I needed to get to my room quickly so that I could feel his tongue in my pussy.

I waved my key quickly, and within seconds we were inside my room. Khalil pulled my skirt up around my waist as soon as he was on the other side of the door. He pushed me forward gently and was anything but gentle when he ripped my panties off in one tug. Khalil took his index finger and slid it across my slippery opening. I turned around and backed up against the hotel dresser for support. Khalil grabbed me by the hair and stuck his tongue in my mouth. He opened my blouse with both hands. My buttons went in opposite directions, making little noises as they hit various surfaces. He took my right breast out of my bra and held it with one hand as he teased my nipple with his tongue. I didn't think my nipples could get any darker or harder, but Khalil seemed to get a kick out of watching them become rock solid under his grip. His other hand played with my pussy. He was so skilled with his finger play. I tried to wiggle out of his grip. I was feeling all kinds of explosions. I could feel my heart racing. When I felt his finger slow down, I opened my eyes, only to find Khalil on his knees.

"I've wanted to taste you since I laid eyes on you." Khalil grasped both thighs, pulling them apart widely so that he could have all access. I leaned back on the dresser as I opened my legs wide for his viewing and tasting pleasure.

I involuntarily threw my head back as his tongue hit my clit. It was strong and deliberate. His tongue felt like one of the best vibrators I've ever owned. He sucked on my clit as he finger fucked me into oblivion.

"I. Can't. Take. It. Ohhh, oooh, baby! Damn, yes!" I moaned as he increased the speed of both his mouth and hand. The simultaneous stimulation had me losing all of my body's hydration. When I couldn't hold on any longer, I succumbed to a body-numbing orgasm that resulted in Khalil drinking a mouthful of me.

"Damn, baby. You tasted better than I expected." Khalil stood up. His dick was protruding to the left of his slacks. The top created a bump in his belt buckle begging to be released. I grabbed his belt buckle ready to release him. I was still panting out of breath from my release, but I knew the sap from his log was just what I needed to give me my wind back. I pulled his pants and boxers down in one swoop, and his massive, black dick sprung forward. It was long and thick. I can usually surmise a man's size in one glance, and while I thought Khalil was packing, I hadn't expected it to be quite that juicy and thick.

"Damn," I said out loud pleased at what I saw. Khalil pulled his shirt over his head, and I took that as my opportunity to run my hands up and down his six-pack. Khalil's eyes were low as he backed me up slowly toward the king-sized bed. Khalil pulled my skirt down from my around my waist and reached behind me and unzipped it. He pulled it down, and I stepped out of it, kicking it aside. Khalil kissed me deeply as he unhooked my bra from the front. My two C-cups spilled out and bounced forward. My nipples were standing at attention, waiting for his touch. They didn't have to wait but a few seconds as he used both of his hands, each gripping a breast and pinching a nipple just rough enough to make my pussy pulsate.

Khalil pushed me down on the bed and pulled my left leg up on his shoulder and began placing kisses on my ankle and calf muscle. He gripped his thick shaft, and just as he was about to put it in, we both paused. I didn't pack condoms, and from the look in his face, I could tell he hadn't brought any to dinner.

Khalil sighed before speaking. "Damn, baby, I don't have any protection. Do you?"

"I usually don't leave home without them," I said breathlessly. I was about to be fucking frustrated! My pussy's throbbing. I have this thick, delicious dick in front of me. The dick is attached to a man who's fine and smart. No condoms? What the fuck was I thinking!

Khalil gently put my leg down from his shoulder and lay on the bed next to me. His dick was still standing at high noon. I looked over at his dick all beautiful and shit. I positioned myself over Khalil and began kissing my way down to his shaft. I gripped it and began stroking it slowly as I looked in his dreamy eyes. The smallest droplet of precum made its way to the surface, and I took that as my cue to taste him. I stuffed his dick in my mouth, covering as much of his shaft as I could, and I pulled it out of my mouth slowly as I flicked my tongue against the backside of the head of his dick. I could see a thin trail of my saliva connecting my lips to his dick as I watched Khalil start to squirm under my grip. I began sucking again; this time speeding up my pace. My jaws were sunken as I used my right hand to stroke the part of his dick that my mouth couldn't cover. I released his dick and placed my mouth on his balls, which had drawn close to his body. I sucked each one and then put them both in my mouth, moving my tongue from one to the other. Khalil had a hold of my hair. His grip was strong as he held on for dear life. I put his dick back in my mouth and continued to suck, determined to get the juice that would satiate me. Khalil held my hair and head and fucked my head as I sucked his dick. I could hear him mumbling some words as his pace quickened. I thought I would choke because of how far his shaft was penetrating my throat.

Then I felt it… A shot of warm liquid filled my mouth as I heard Khalil yell, "Wyn! Wyn! Ahhh, fuck!" His body shuddered and then it relaxed.

I kissed him on the lips and got up to go rinse my mouth in the bathroom. I looked at myself in the mirror. My hair was a mess, but I don't think I'd ever felt sexier. When I walked out of the bathroom, I found Khalil under the sheets snoring. I crawled into the bed beside him, and just when I started to turn over away from him to snooze, he embraced me in a spooning position, and we both fell off to sleep.

I picked up the hotel phone and thanked the concierge for my wake-up call. It was an early and short day with a closing breakfast and then my return to Atlanta. I turned to see Khalil still asleep as handsome as he was when he's awake. I decided to brush my teeth and shower before waking him. I actually hated that I hated to go. I don't know why I was even feeling any type of way. Shit, I hadn't even gotten my back broke by him yet. I could hear the water running in the sink, and I peeked out to see a naked Khalil gargling with my mouthwash. Just as I was rinsing the suds from my body, he opened the shower curtain and stepped in. I hadn't taken a shower with anyone in years—it wasn't really my thing. I enjoyed the privacy that a shower brought, but when Khalil stepped in and I felt his skin on my back, the need to have him near me was more important than my privacy. Especially knowing that I would probably not make his acquaintance again.

Khalil began moving his hands up and down the sides of my arms and then over my behind. He placed kisses along my shoulder blade as the warm water bounced on his head and down his back. I took the opportunity to lather up my hands with the shower gel as I turned around and began a slow massage of soap and water on his pecs, arms, and shoulders. I took the suds from my hands and stroked his already engorged penis in my hands, making sure I didn't miss a millimeter with my sudsy touch. Khalil held his head back and had his eyes closed as I offered slow, cleansing strokes. When I thought he was thoroughly clean, I gently nudged him toward the waiting stream of water. I watched him turn a few times, seemingly enjoying the warm stream flowing over his brown skin, washing the suds away. When Khalil opened his eyes and stopped moving, he just stood still and stared in my eyes. I felt really naked as his eyes penetrated me. Khalil grabbed me by the back of my wet hair and stuck his tongue in my mouth.

His hands began to roam my body, and when they landed on my ass, he squeezed each cheek tightly, pulling me closer to his wet body. His dick was pressed up against my stomach as we kissed with a passion that was unfamiliar to me. Before I could protest, he picked up my right leg and guided himself inside of me. I let out a groan as he widened my opening. Khalil met my groan with his own moans and mumblings.

"Shit, Wynter. Shit!" he whispered as he began a slow pump inside of my flooded walls.

I hadn't had unprotected sex in decades, and his dick melted into me and offered a feeling that was unexplainable. Khalil kissed my neck as he pumped himself in me so deep I thought we would become one. As he gripped one breast in his free hand and the other on my leg that was wrapped around his waist, I tried to steady myself in the unfamiliar hotel shower against the wall. I moved in sync with his grind, wanting to feel every throbbing vein in his thick shaft inside of me. I was so caught up in the pleasure I was feeling from the nerves that were on end between my legs to the nerves that were tingling on my lips, creating what seemed to be an invisible, magnetic feel from his mouth to mine. In retrospect, it's hard to explain. My lips had never felt a sensation like that when kissing anyone else, and trust me, I've kissed my share of men.

Khalil put my leg down and spun me around, and I bent over knowing what we both wanted. I arched my back as Khalil sank in slowly. He let out a groan.

"Damn, this shit feels good, baby," I replied with my own moans letting him know that I was feeling it too.

When he reached around my waist and began to rub my swollen clit, which caused my pussy to reach its point of explosion. My walls contracted and released as I came all over his shaft.

My contracting tunnel must've been like a milking for him as he yelped, "Argggh, shit!"

My insides filled up quickly with the warm fluid from his body. Khalil reluctantly eased himself out of me and pulled me up to a standing position. We faced each other, both seeming to be coming down from our high, realizing what we had just done.

Before I could speak, Khalil kissed me while backing me under the water for my rinse off. He took the showerhead down and sprayed it on my gushy opening. I took it from him, spraying my opening, hoping to wash all of his seeping juices out of me knowing full well that wasn't possible. After I cleaned myself off again, I stepped out of the shower, leaving him to finish bathing.

I felt light on my feet. My orgasm gave me the jolt I needed in making the trip to New York worth it.

Khalil got dressed in last evening's outfit quickly and made his way to his room with promises to see me before we each left to return to our lives. When he left my room, I didn't give myself much time to think about what we had done. I still had to blow-dry my hair and apply my makeup before getting dressed. I rushed around my room, packing up my toiletries and ensuring I had all of my suits out of the hotel closet and packed up neatly. I got dressed in a simple skinny, black, ankle-length pantsuit. I was looking forward to getting back to the milder Atlanta weather.

As the conference breakfast closed, I noticed that I didn't see Khalil. I shrugged it off, thinking maybe it was best if we said our goodbyes in the shower that morning. I made my way to the concierge to get my luggage so that I could jump in a yellow cab and head to JFK. I smelled him.

"You weren't going to leave without seeing me, were you?" Khalil held on to my elbow as he spoke.

"I have your contact info. At least I think I do. Well, let's just say I know how to find you," I responded lightheartedly. "When I didn't see you at the breakfast, I thought I had seen the last of you." I smirked.

Khalil frowned. "The last of me?" He broke his frown and smiled playfully, pointing at himself. "Woman, we're just getting to know each other. You won't be getting away from me quite that easy, Miss Wynter."

"I wasn't trying to get away from you." I blushed. "We live two completely different lives, not to mention two completely different states. It was nice meeting and getting to know you during my time in New York. You definitely made my trip that much more pleasurable." I pecked Khalil on his sweet lips and took in a deep whiff of the aftershave that lingered in his beard. Khalil winked at me.

"I'll be in touch, Wynter. Safe travels."

I leaned back in my first-class seat, listening to the white-haired man next to me snore. As soon as he sat down, he threw back three complimentary bottles of Skyy Vodka and dozed off to a loud sleep. I put on my headphones and decided to listen to some R&B music. Every song seemed to put me in the mind-set to fuck Khalil again. Even if it was just one more time. I thought about how smooth his bald head felt under my palm as his tongue played with my pulsating, fleshy mound. No doubt about it; he definitely had skills. Many men think just because they go down there and open their mouths that they're doing something, when in fact, more often than not, I'm thinking, *Just put your dick in so I can at least get some pleasure because what you're doing right now ain't it.*

Just as I was about to doze off, the pilot announced that we would be landing soon, and I couldn't be happier. Mr. Snorer was snorting and mumbling to himself so much in his sleep that my music couldn't even drown it out. I grabbed my luggage and jumped in my waiting car service, thankful for my secretary and her planning. As soon as I sat in the car service, my phone started buzzing. I assumed it was one or all of my girls texting me knowing I was due home today.

K: You made it to the A safely?

I blushed, glad that no one was looking as I smiled sillily at my phone. I started not to answer him right away. I didn't need him getting any ideas like I was eager to hear from him, but I responded anyway. I didn't want him to be worried. That's what I told myself.

Me: I'm safe. In car service on my way home. Thanks for checking. You made it to Jacksonville already?

His response was quick.

K: No, I'm actually about to board now. I had a few NY errands to run before I left the big city.

Me: Cool. Well thanks for checking on me.

I put my phone back in my purse, determined not to keep carrying on a conversation with him. New York was fun, but it was time for me to get back to business.

I had the car service stop by the pharmacy before taking me to my place. I needed to pick up some emergency contraception to put an end to the possibility of a pregnancy before it got started. Once home, I settled in and decided to make an OB-GYN appointment as well as catch up on some work-related emails before I did anything else. After checking my emails, I looked at my phone to find eight new messages—four of which from Khalil, and the others from my girls. I responded to my besties, letting them know that I was good to meet up with them for dinner and drinks at eight, but only Spree was free for the evening, so I told her I would meet with her. I put my phone facedown on my marble tabletop, but then I picked it up and decided to read his messages.

K: Hey, baby. I've landed safely.

K: Baby, I can't stop thinking about you.

K: Call me when you can. I want to hear your voice.

K: Don't be trying to avoid me, Wynter. You already know what it is.

I wasn't sure if I should be flattered or worried that his ass was a stalker. Then I thought about how smooth, smart, delicious, and delectable Khalil was, and I knew he didn't have the need to stalk anyone. Not even me.

I pressed call and waited to hear the deep baritone voice of my one-night lover. "So you called."

"How are you? How was your flight?" I wasn't the best at small talk. I didn't find much use for it.

"My flight was fine. I'm better now that I'm hearing from you. I was hoping that you would call me, because if you didn't, I was going to call you."

"Well, it was really nice meeting you at the conference. I enjoyed our evening and morning together." I giggled.

"Not more than me. You're a very beautiful woman, Wynter. I'm sure you already know that. You're smart too, and that's a real turn-on. I'm interested in learning you."

"Learning me? I don't think that's possible. I like you, K. You're a great guy. You're handsome and successful. I'm sure you have women at your beck and call. I live in Atlanta, and you're in Jacksonville. Let's enjoy the time we had and be thankful for making each other's acquaintance."

The phone was silent for a few seconds.

"You're acting like Jacksonville and Atlanta are on opposite sides of the country. People make long-distance relationships work every day."

I moved the phone from my ear and looked at it for a second before speaking.

"Relationship? Listen, I'm not looking for any relationship kind of setup, Khalil. That's not really my thing. I like you. I think you're great. I just can't give you a relationship if that's what you're looking for."

"Okay, Wynter. I'll settle for being your friend. How about that?" Khalil was persistent. He didn't know it, but his persistence was turning me on.

"Cool. Friends. Friends with benefits would be even better," I stated.

"You are too much. But if that's all you want, then how can I complain about that?"

"You can't. Anyway, let me get off this phone. I'm supposed to link with one of my sister-friends in a few."

"No problem, Wyn. I'll speak to you again soon." I could hear Khalil huff as he ended the call.

I saw Spree sitting at the bar alone, looking at her phone. I smiled thinking of how much her confidence had grown since we met. "Hey, friend," I said as I pecked her on her cheek and took a seat next to her.

"Hi, pooh! Welcome back from the Big Apple. How was it? I know you got your shopping on!"

I motioned for the waiter. "I'll have a dry martini. Hold the olive." I turned my attention to my friend. "Girl! New York was better than I expected in every way! I did do some shopping. The conference was typical. But child, when I tell you I had some of the best dick I've ever had!"

"Wait, bitch, what?" I watched Spree's face light up. "You just now telling me! Where you get this dick from? Was it coka or ether? Don't hold out on a dick-hungry bitch! Let me know!" Spree exclaimed.

I took a sip of my martini before explaining. "His name is Khalil. Khalil Jameson, and when I say he's fine… sis… This muthafucka is a creamy-brown, bald-headed, and built like a male model. Not to mention his dick game…" I placed my hand over my chest as if I was trying to catch my breath.

"Damn! It was like that?" Spree said as she downed the rest of her drink and motioned the bartender for another.

"So what's his story?" Spree inquired.

"Well, he's divorced. Couple of teenaged kids. An attorney with a successful practice. Claims to be single. But you and I both know. Single means at least two bitches that think they're in a relationship with him." We both laughed.

"True. You think you'll see him again? Shit, I know I would, especially with how scarce a good piece of cock is 'round these parts."

"He seems to be interested in more than just fucking me. You know I don't have time for the okie doke," I said as I finished the last of my martini.

"We all know how you feel about the bullshit these men be pumping. You never know tho. He might be your prince charming," Spree offered.

"You know better than anybody I don't want or need a prince charming. I just need a steady piece to give me shivers. All the rest of the fantasy shit I can do without."

We sat and caught up for a little while longer. Spree still hadn't gotten laid the way she wanted and complained about it over appetizers.

Before I closed my eyes, I thought about Khalil. His scent, his eyes, his tongue, and his touch. Even his conversation was good, meaningful even. I was exhausted from the travel and from hitting the gym after drinks with Spree, but sleep still evaded me. I tossed and turned. Thoughts of Khalil permeated my mind. I picked up the phone and texted him knowing he may have already been deep in REM sleep.

Me: Hey. Thought of you.

I put my phone down and placed a pillow over my face. No one was watching, but for some reason I felt stupid texting him. I was so horny for him. I closed my eyes and began to rub my nipples over my satin chemise. My nipples were as hard as they could get as I imagined his tongue flickering, taking turns on each breast. I slid my right hand down from the nipple it was tweaking, past my waist, and pulled up my chemise. I put my hand in my panties, and just as I was about to touch my throbbing clit, I heard my phone go off, interrupting my sexy thoughts of him.

I picked up my phone quickly.

K: Hey what are you doing up? I thought you'd be getting your beauty sleep. You're thinking about me, and I haven't stopped thinking about you. What's on your mind? Can you talk?

I dialed Khalil's number, and he answered on the second ring.

"Baby."

"Did I wake you? I was up later than usual and wanted to hear your voice," I said.

"No. I actually just got off the phone with my great-aunty. She has some documents she wants me to review for her regarding her estate. I'm going to take a quick trip out there to see her on Friday. She lives in Powder Springs. I was hoping I could take you out to dinner while I'm in town."

"Powder Springs? Oh okay. That's a little over a half hour from me. My place is in Decatur if you don't mind driving a little." I was trying to contain my excitement.

"That's nothing. I can't wait to see you, baby."

We talked for almost an hour about everything. His daughters, his ex-wife, his practice. I learned that he lived close to his ex so that he could play an active role in his girls' lives and that he saw them a few times a week.

Friday evening couldn't come fast enough. I rushed out of the office, waving bye to my secretary before she could stop me for Friday afternoon small talk. "Have a great weekend! See you Monday!" I sang as I walked out. I had an appointment scheduled with my hair girl. Just a simple wash and set was all I needed to get me right. After I was finished at the salon, I swung by the florist to pick up some fresh sunflowers and headed home. Downtown Atlanta rush-hour traffic was crazy, especially on a Friday evening.

"I'm expecting a guest—Mr. Jameson. You can send him up when he arrives," I told my doorman.

"Very well, Ms. Williams," Otis said as he tipped his hat in my direction.

I put my Pandora on to the Sade station, lit two of the eucalyptus-mint aromatherapy candles that were bestsellers from Fallon's Relax-With-Me Spa line. I pulled out a simple black, strapless, fitted ankle-length Givenchy jumpsuit. I had been waiting for the right occasion to pull it out, and tonight seemed appropriate. I showered and went light on the makeup. A little brow fill, a touch of highlight on my cheeks, and a nice brick-brown nude lipstick for my pout. I unwrapped my hair, and it fell to my shoulders. I shook my head a little from side to side, and my hair fell right into place. I swayed my hips along to the beat of Sade's "Sweetest Taboo". It was something soothing and sexy about her voice that just put me in a sultry mood. I heard my intercom buzz, and I knew it was Otis calling to let me know that Khalil was on his way up. When my bell rang, my heart pounded, and my stomach fluttered. I hadn't let anyone make me feel this nervous, not ever.

I gave myself a quick pep talk before I opened the door.

"Welcome to my humble abode," I said as I opened the door for him to enter. Khalil grabbed me in the tightest embrace and planted a long, wet kiss on my lips.

"I've been waiting to do that shit all week. Damn, Wynter, you don't disappoint."

I took in Khalil. He smelled as delicious as he had when I last saw him. He was dressed casually in a pair of dark jeans, white V-neck Polo T-shirt, and black blazer.

"I concur," I said after I caught my breath.

"Sade Adu. Classic. One of my favorites actually. She's on my playlist for my road trips. You have a beautiful place here. Nice piano. You play?" Khalil asked as he took in my space.

"I took piano lessons back in North Carolina before we moved to Atlanta," I said as I quickly thought back to my life before we moved to Atlanta, and shit went crazy. I wiped my hand over the smooth, cool surface of my white baby grand piano before losing my train of thought. "So what are we getting into tonight?"

"I have reservations for us at the Atlas," he said.

"That's probably the one place in Atlanta that I haven't eaten."

"Even better then. I'm ready when you are," Khalil said as he reached for my hand.

I smiled as he took my hand and led me toward the door.

Dinner was fabulous, but our dinner conversation was even better. Khalil had no problem keeping his eyes on me, even with some of the most beautiful women sauntering around the restaurant. I was happy to be at the restaurant with Khalil, but my panties were becoming increasingly more moist the longer we sat there. After dinner we headed back to my place, and when we got to my door Khalil kissed me.

"I'm going to be here all weekend. I'd love to see you again tomorrow."

"You're not coming in? Oh, fuck, you're coming in," I said as I pulled Khalil in by the hem of his blazer. He didn't protest.

We locked lips, undressing our way through my living room. I felt Khalil's erection pressed up against my stomach as we kissed. It felt warm, hard, and thick. Khalil picked me up and carried me over to my piano and lay me down. He sat on the bench and spread my legs open in front of him. He took two of his fingers and held my pussy open as he placed his mouth over my clit and began to suck. At first it was light pressure, but then he increased the pressure, sucking my clit with a force better than my best vibrator. He flicked his tongue, adjusting the pressure until my feet pounded the piano keys playing a tune that no one wanted to hear. My pelvis lifted as I grinded against his mouth, finishing my explosion. He sucked and slurped, thirsty for the juices I released. I lay on my back panting, trying to catch my breath and then I felt my legs go up. Khalil picked me up from the piano and placed my legs on his shoulders. He held me like I was light as a feather as he pushed his dick in my oozing opening.

"Awww, shit! You been waiting for this dick?" he asked through gritted teeth as he pumped in me.

I could feel my orgasm building again as I moaned, "Oooh, yeah! You feel so fucking good."

Khalil carried me to my bed and laid me down. He got on top of me and began to move slow, kissing my neck and sucking my breasts one at a time. He kissed my lips so passionately. I thought he would melt in me that's how good and deep he felt. Khalil kissed my forehead and began to pick up speed. I could feel a tingle inside of me as if the tip of his dick was connected to my cervix.

Khalil's lips were close to my ears as he whispered, "Damn, I love this pussy." Khalil jerked and pulled out, spraying his warm, thick liquid on my sweaty belly. When his dick finished pulsating,

Khalil rolled off of me onto his back, attempting to catch his breath. "I'll get something to wipe you with." He heaved.

"No, baby, it's okay. I got it. Relax," I said as I got up to go get some damp towels to wipe us both down with.

We made love two more times that night. Each time unexpectedly better than the next. I didn't think that was possible. As the morning approached, I got up to brush my teeth and freshen up before I got back in the bed. I watched Khalil sleep, and for once, I wasn't ready to kick him out of my bed or my house. We spent the entire weekend together shopping for ourselves, and he picked up a few things for his daughters. We got to talk. It was weird and scary. I actually liked being around him; it was unnerving.

"Well, Mr. K has been coming to town every week for the past two months I see. Somebody's got that ether!" Summer teased as she bit into a carrot. Lunch with her was always a good way to break up my day.

"Yeah, he has. I don't know what to make of it. He wants me to come to Jacksonville this weekend, but I don't know if I'm ready," I said.

"Why the hell not? Sis, you finally met a dude you like for more than a roll in the sack. You better follow up on that shit."

"That's the problem. I don't like feeling like this. You know I don't like allowing anyone the power to have control of my emotions. Fuckers get you all open, and then they start doing stupid shit. I'm on the right side of the law and I'd like to stay that way, but the way these mothafuckas act, they will have you ready to kill they ass," I said seriously.

"I know, sis. But you are allowed to fall in love sometime. What you're feeling now, I felt once, and I don't know if I'll ever experience that again. Good dudes don't come by often, so grab that shit while you got it." Summer pouted as she reflected.

"Who's really good though? They are all good at the start of the relationship, and then they get bored and start doing fucked-up shit," I said as I rolled my eyes.

"True. It happens like that a lot of the time. But not all the time, Wyn. All I'm saying is I've never seen you this open off of anybody, ever. If he has what it takes to keep your attention this far, then I think you should give him the opportunity to prove himself. That is all." Summer countered.

"I guess you're right, little sis. I'll keep that in mind."

Khalil offered to fly me out to Jacksonville, but I opted to take the five-hour drive, hoping that the drive would give me time to think and calm my nerves. I pulled up to the development he lived in and was immediately impressed. All modern, ranch-style homes on tree-lined streets forming one looping cul-de-sac after the other. I pulled into his driveway and thought I would have a second to calm my nerves before I got out. Just as I turned the car off, the front door opened, and two long-legged, chocolate beauties walked out. They rushed over to the car—one with her hair blown straight and hanging just below her shoulders, and the other with a high ponytail that swayed with every step she took. They both had large, round, brown eyes similar to Khalil's, so I knew right away that they were his daughters. I took a deep breath and got out.

"Hi! You must be Wynter. I'm Kassidy, and this is my sister Kennedy," she said as she smiled, exposing her braces.

"Yes, I'm Wynter. It's very nice to meet you both. I expected you young ladies to be pretty, but I had no idea you would both be so gorgeous!" They both giggled.

"You're very pretty yourself, Miss Wynter," Kennedy offered.

The two teen girls were really gorgeous with their pouty, gloss-covered lips and button noses. Just as I was about to walk toward the front door, it swung open, and Khalil came out and embraced me in a hug that swept me off my feet.

"I see you met the girls! They were waiting for you to get here before they left."

"Yes. They introduced themselves."

"Let me get your bags from the car," Khalil said as he rushed over to my car.

I stood in the doorway of his sunlit foyer admiring his décor—simple, clean, and neat in neutral tones. The marble floor shined under my sandals.

"We'll see you before you leave, Miss Wynter," Kassidy said as both girls waved goodbye.

"What are you guys doing this evening? Can you join your father and I for dinner?" I saw a smile spread across their faces as well as Khalil's. They looked at their father before answering. His smile let them know it was well with him.

"Sure! That would be super!" Kennedy cheered.

"We'll pick you guys up around seven. Be ready, and don't pile all that shit on your faces." Khalil joked.

"Whatever, Dad!" Kassidy said as she and Kennedy made their way to a cute, blue late-model Toyota Camry.

We walked in the house, and Khalil showed me around. Three bedrooms, four bathrooms, an eat-in kitchen, and dining room that extended to an open living room—all in colors of the fall: browns, burgundy, burnt-orange, and tan. The skylights throughout his house made it exceptionally bright and airy.

"Are you hungry, babe? I have some appetizers waiting for you," Khalil said as he led me to the kitchen by the hand.

"You didn't have to! I'm fine. But this spread looks too good to not eat." I joked.

"I just want you to be comfortable. Make yourself at home please. You've been so welcoming in sharing your space with me when I'm in your neck of the woods. I just want to do the same and more if you'll let me," Khalil said seriously.

"K, you know this is more than I've done with a man in a while. But here I am."

"I know, Wyn. I know how resistant you've been to all of this. Every time I push, you pull. I know you may not know what to do with my lovin', but I'm prepared to show you that I ain't going nowhere. I told you that I'm not like every other dude out there. My wife and I divorced, but not because of infidelity. We got together young, and we grew apart. I'm not trying to rush you into anything, but I have to tell you I fell for you the first night we sat in that little lounge in the city."

I looked in his eyes, searching for a hint of deception. I hadn't been able to find any bullshit in him since the day we met. I just couldn't bring myself to let my heart be vulnerable enough to be held in anyone else's hand.

"Let's just take it one day at a time. I'm here, and that's a big step. Shit, I'm met your daughters! That's big for me"

"One day at a time, baby. I'll take it one second at a time. Anything you need," Khalil said as he planted a wet kiss on my lips.

Dinner with his daughters was better than I expected. We had a lot in common. The young girls were both interested in law like their father. I saw some of my young ambition in their eyes, and that felt great. After dinner, we went for ice cream before dropping them at home. When we got to Khalil's place, he pressed a few buttons on the remote to his sound system, and Sade's sweet voice came blaring through the speakers. He opened a bottle of my favorite red wine and poured me a glass.

"Sit back. Relax. I'll be back in a few," Khalil said as he disappeared toward the back of the house.

I was just about finished with my glass of wine when I smelled the relaxing scent of mint and eucalyptus in the air. Khalil rushed into the living room rubbing his hands together.

"Okay, baby, follow me," he said as he extended his hand out to me.

As we walked toward the back of his home, he got behind me and held me closely. I felt his lips on my neck. His warm kisses sent a chill up my spine. Well, that and the hard lump I felt pressed against my ass. As my favorite scent got stronger, my eyes lit up. He had the Jacuzzi going in his screened-in back porch. It was bubbling with small scented candles lining the entire closed-in area and a bucket of champagne on ice along the Jacuzzi.

"Wow!" I said. My eyes were wide with surprise. Khalil didn't say a word.

I watched him pull his shirt over his head and pull his pants down, and I did the same. Khalil unhooked my bra, and I stepped out of my sandals. He pulled my pants and panties down together. I did a sensuous twirl for him, giving him a moment to take in the curve of my hips, the round of my ass, and the bounce of my tits. Khalil stepped back and watched me while shaking his head and licking his lips.

"Girl, you just don't know," he said.

"I don't know what?"

"Get your behind in that water so I can show you what," he demanded.

I sank into the warm water and pulled my hair up into a messy bun before closing my eyes and letting my head fall back against the headrest. Between the heat and massaging jets that were blowing against my back, the soothing sounds of The Weeknd crooning out "You Earned It", and the smell of the candles in the air, I didn't think I could feel any more relaxed or content.

My eyes rolled back as I felt the pressure of his finger against my clit. He was massaging it in slow circles. I instinctively parted my legs wider to ensure there would be no reason for him to stop. My lips parted and formed a circle as I let a moan escape. I opened my eyes when the coolness hit my right leg as it was lifted above the warm water. Khalil was skilled. The pressure on my clit didn't cease as he placed my big toe in his mouth. It felt electric as every nerve from the tip of my toes to the top of my head danced. I exploded with my body jerking as my juices joined the Jacuzzi water we sat in.

When my body stopped moving, I opened my eyes to see a sexy smirk on Khalil's face. He pulled me to him as he sat against the Jacuzzi. I wrapped my legs around his waist as he lowered me onto the log waiting between his legs. As my opening stretched as he expanded me, I could hear his breathing deepen as his heart beat rapidly against my breast. I placed my tongue in his mouth as our tongues met our thrusts. We were in a heated competition. I'd thrust my hips against him, letting him know that I could handle it, his thickness, and his length. Khalil held my waist. The water made me weightless as he moved his hips to meet mine. We were both sweating profusely from the steam and the heat we created between us. I reached over his shoulder and grabbed a piece of ice from the champagne bucket. I put it in my mouth and exchanged it with him. We sucked the ice simultaneously until it disappeared between our lips. I bounced relentlessly. My clit throbbed, enjoying the grind against him I was getting. Khalil held my waist and tried to slow the inevitable, but I wasn't having it. I shifted his dick inside me, moving my hips to the left and then the right.

"Damn, baby. I don't want to cummm…"

Those were the last words he said before I saw his mouth contort, straining to hold his seed. I felt the liquid shoot in me like a warm douche. I bounced, contracting my walls, milking his dick until it was empty, and his eyes opened.

My drive back to Atlanta had me deep in thought. I had the best time I ever had with any man in my more than three decades on this earth. Khalil gave me something I never thought I'd ever want— a relationship. I heard my phone ring as I saw the sign welcoming me back to Georgia.

"Fallon! Sissy, what's good?" I exclaimed as I pressed the answer button on my car's screen.

"You tell me, baby girl! You been making moves with homeboy I see."

"Yeah. I'm just hitting the peach. We got to link with the girls. I got a story to tell!" I giggled.

"Really? Let me find out Miss I Don't Need A Man For Nothing But The Dick feeling like she wants more." Fallon pressed.

"We got a ways to go, but he's definitely someone I can be around for more than twenty-four. You know that's saying a lot. Enough about me. You good?"

"I'm okay—still trying to get where you are, but I guess we all have our season," Fallon said, sounding encouraged.

Spree

I had just had a date with yet another gonna be, wanna be music exec. I ended the date after appetizers and acted like I was leaving, but I just went to the bathroom to reapply my lipstick while waiting for him to go. My dating life was in shambles. I made my way back to the bar of the hotel restaurant and sat down.

"Hey, weren't you just here?" the cute, young bartender asked as he sat the cocktail menu down in front of me.

"Yeah. I'm back." I mumbled as I ordered another set of wings and my favorite, Blue Bellini. All of my dating and then post-date eating was undoing what I had done cosmetically. I had gained ten pounds all in my hips, and my fupa was on swole. I pulled out my phone and started scrolling through Instagram as I sipped my drink. I paused when I saw a picture of Wynter and her boyfriend Khalil, smiling with white sand and crystal-clear water behind them. They were on yet another baecation in the Caribbean. Seeing the smile on Wynter's face made me smile knowing that she seemed to have found her ecstasy. Meanwhile, my most recent moments of ecstasy had been self-induced. A little Pornhub, a little wine, and my index finger, and I'm good for a mini explosion. It gets the job done, but I would like to feel some warm hands and a set of lips on me from time to time. I was interrupted out of my thoughts by the sound of a deep voice.

"Is anyone sitting here?"

I looked from his feet to his head. Damn! Average height, pair of brown Ferragamos, tan pants, MCM belt, white button-up shirt, goatee, chocolate skin, deep-slanted, pitch-black eyes, and low waves.

I gave him my sexiest look as I responded, "You're sitting here." I patted the seat.

I saw his pearly white teeth as he chuckled slightly. "Thanks."

Just as I was about to introduce myself, I heard, "Honey did you find us seats?"

I turned to look and took her in too from foot to head. She was wearing Miu Miu crystal shoes, short David Koma leather skirt, and a cropped cream top exposing her flat stomach, and I instantly sucked in mine. Two carats were on her left hand. She had French-manicured nails, creamy-butterscotch skin, bright-red, filler-plumped dick-suckling lips, and blunt-cut, jet-black hair. She was pretty and vaguely familiar. I wanted to roll my eyes, but I didn't.

"Yeah, this young lady was gracious enough to save us two seats," he said. I guess that was his version of a joke.

I turned my back slightly and went back to scrolling through other people's lives on social media as they took their seats. I bit into my crispy chicken wings, the sweet-honey hot sauce that coated them was sticking to my fingers. I was watching an Instagram video

Summer posted showing her new haircut. I shrieked in disbelief looking at my sis without her long, blonde locks. I couldn't believe she let her hair go. She looked like a naturally-blonde Amber Rose now.

"You okay over there?" the woman who was sitting next to Mr. Dreamy asked.

I looked over at her quizzically. I didn't think I was that loud.

"Yes, I'm fine. Sorry if I disturbed you two," I said, dabbing the corners of my mouth, hoping I didn't look like Ronald McDonald from the sauce.

"You didn't disturb us," he said, showing his dimples and pearly whites again.

Ralph Angel, I thought to myself. He reminds me of Ralph Angel from that show *Queen Sugar*.

"Are you waiting for guests? Can we offer you a drink?" He was sweet.

"Um, no, that's okay. I was actually just getting myself ready to leave." I lied.

"Leave? The night's still young. Let me get you a drink. We were just waiting for our table. Why don't you join us?" the woman asked.

I blushed. "I don't know if you see this plate in front of me, but I just killed these wings. Thank you for the invite though."

Damn, did I look that lonely?

"If you don't have any prior engagements you have to be at, we won't take no for an answer," the sexy man said.

I smiled and thought to myself, *Hey, why not? I'm just going home to eat ice cream and Netflix and chill alone. What could it hurt?*

I followed them over to their table as the woman told the waiter that it would be three now instead of two.

"How is it that we're about to have dinner but have yet to formally introduce ourselves? I'm Omari, and this is my fiancée, Kris." Kris extended her pretty, dainty hand in my direction.

"I'm Spree. It's nice to meet you both. Thank you for allowing me to barge in on your dinner. I really was just about to leave."

"We love company. So it's our pleasure," Kris said.

We took our seats, and after the initial pleasantries were over, we took time talking about ourselves. I told them that I was a divorcée and still hadn't figured out what I wanted to do with my life yet. I learned that Kris was originally from Oakland, California and that she and Omari met when she relocated to Atlanta for work. She was an actress and was on a show that filmed out of an Atlanta studio. Omari was a set director and had been working in television and film for almost a decade.

I didn't eat. I picked over a salad as I watched them eat, feeding each other while cooing. I felt like a voyeur watching them in an intimate moment. The drinks were flowing. Omari ordered round after round as our glasses were filled the moment they looked like they were about to be empty. We exchanged contact information and laughed about everything from social media blogs to the characters on reality TV. It was getting late, so I decided I better get going.

"You guys have been great, but I had better get going. How much can I give you toward the bill?"

"Don't be silly! It was our treat! Please consider yourself a friend of ours," Kris said.

"You're too sweet. I better get going. I've intruded enough for the evening." I stood up to excuse myself and stumbled a bit, not realizing the alcohol that I consumed had taken effect.

"You can't drive in your condition," O stated as he grabbed my elbow to ensure I was steady.

"I can order an Uber. That's what I'll do," I insisted.

"You won't do anything of the sort. We have a room upstairs. You'll come up there and sleep it off. Then you can drive your car home in the morning," Kris demanded.

"No, I don't think so. Thank you for the offer, really, but I better be getting home." I opened my Uber app.

"Okay, I tell you what. Come upstairs, and sit a little while. We have a suite, so you won't be crowding our space. You really can't even trust some of these strange Uber drivers when you're inebriated." O made a convincing plea. Besides, he was so fine how could I say no to his offer?

"Alright. As long as I'm not impeding." I was glad for their company.

We made our way up to their suite; a one-bedroom, two-bathroom room with a living room and full kitchen in the swanky hotel.

I excused myself to the bathroom to relieve my bladder and to rinse my mouth. It was a habit of mine.

When I exited the bathroom, I could hear Ciara blasting as Kris stood in the living room reenacting Ciara's dance to her hit song "Level Up". Kris danced seductively as she popped her thin pelvis and acted up. Omari was filling up three flutes with Dom P as he shuffled to the music.

"Dance with me!" Kris said as she pulled me to dance with her.

I wasn't one to be shy, and the alcohol ended any chance of me playing bashful. I pumped my pelvis. My expensive jeans were not up for the challenge my round ass was giving. Kris grabbed my hands and held them up in the air as we both danced clumsily, giggling like young girls.

O handed us each a glass, and we all toasted as we danced like a trio of old friends. I spun and danced, drinking down my bubbly feeling carefree. I kicked off my shoes like it was my room and began to dance seductively as Ella Mai poured her heart out that she was trippin'. I saw O watching me hungrily as he whispered in Kris's ear. She was watching me too. I saw a sly smile spread across her face as O whispered.

I waved my finger, admonishing them. "No, no. No secrets. If I'm your guest, then you shouldn't be keeping secrets."

O smiled. "I was actually just admiring you and telling Kris how beautiful you are."

I looked at Kris, trying to read her face to see if she was upset about what he just said.

"I told him I thought you were beautiful from the moment I saw you sitting at the bar." Kris smirked.

I was drunk, but I still blushed at the compliments they were giving me.

"Thank you. You guys don't have to feel sorry for the drunk girl who's become your entertainment for the evening."

Kris walked over to me and pulled me close as she danced slowly with me. She traced her hands up and down my hips slowly. I felt stunned at first. The five seconds I spent confused were replaced by a weird feeling. I wasn't sure why I hadn't removed myself from her embrace. She tilted my chin up and moved her tongue across my lips.

"Honey, she tastes as good as she looks," Kris called out to O, who sat lustfully watching the display from the couch.

"I knew she would. Taste some more," he commanded.

Kris preceded to kiss me with an open mouth, and I returned the tongue. When I felt her hands cup my breasts, I flinched but just for a moment before I let go and sank into the feeling. I was unsure what to do with my hands, so I did the same. I cupped her large, solid breasts. Her nipples were hard. I assumed she had breast implants because her breasts felt like mine. My eyes were closed, and I was into it, enjoying the feel of her soft lips and hot tongue. I almost forgot O was there until I felt another set of lips on the back of my neck and a hard dick on my ass.

Kris unbuttoned my shirt, and Omari took it off of me. Kris unzipped my jeans, and O pulled them down, getting on his knees behind me I could feel his face against my bare ass. Kris stepped back and peeled out of her clothes with her gaze steady on me. I had to admit, she was built beautifully. Her body was statuesque, perfectly toned, and tight. She stepped out of her skirt and tossed her panties toward me and her fiancé, who was undoing his belt buckle. Kris was still in her heels as she walked toward the bedroom. She turned to me just as she reached the French doors that led to the room and finger waved for me to follow her. I did.

Kris was positioned with her knees bent behind her as she pulled me toward her. I was standing in front of the bed when she took her two fingers and slid them between my legs.

"Oh, you're wet already, and I'm thirsty." She purred.

She pulled the covers back and pulled me down. My back fell against the cool, crisp sheets. I opened my legs as she kissed her way down my stomach. I saw Omari watching. His more than average-sized dick was in his hands, and he stroked slowly. I closed my eyes as her tongue parted my pussy lips into a smile. Unlike with a man, it didn't take her several licks to find my spot. Her tongue hit my clit with the right pressure. She cupped her mouth around my mound of flesh and worked it in circles. I held her head and enjoyed the sensation building between my thighs. When I opened my eyes, I saw Omari deep in her, pumping eagerly as he watched her devour my pussy. I was so turned on… more turned on than I had been in years. I exploded just as Omari pulled his dick out of Kris and came on my breast.

I came four times that night. Four times! Some of the scenes were a blur. At different points, our three bodies intertwined in some positions I still don't know how we managed. I sucked Omari, he fed me his dick, and I downed it… all eight inches. I even tasted Kris's honey pot. Scentless. It tasted better than I ever thought a pussy could taste. I woke up the next morning and looked at my new friends… my lovers. My head was spinning and pounding from the liquor and sexcapade the night before, but I managed to find my clothes and put them on without waking the two. I crept toward the door and made my out the hotel and to my car. I sat in my car for about ten minutes before pulling off. I looked at myself in my rearview mirror. I couldn't believe the act I took part in. When I got home, I jumped in the shower, attempting to rinse any trace of them off of me. I don't know what got into me, but I knew I couldn't let it happen again.

A few weeks had gone by without a word from either of my two one-night stands. I had been watching Oprah's network when I saw her grace the screen. *She's much thinner than that in person*, I thought to myself as I bit into a piece of the lemon cake I had baked earlier that day. I had thought back to that evening several times since it happened. Sometimes I thought I should've declined their offer to sit with them at dinner, and other times, when a wave of horniness came over me, I replay the parts of the night that I can recollect blow by blow, lick by lick, and suck by suck. The thoughts of that night have been helpful in giving me the explosive self-induced orgasms that even Pornhub couldn't. I looked at the clock and realized I had better be heading out. I had plans to meet Fallon for an early dinner.

I had just had my hair cornrowed in long, blonde braids that went straight back and touched the top of my ass. I put a little edge gel to taper down my hairs, applied a pretty, soft-pink lip gloss, threw on my shades, and jogged out to my car. I was always the one who was late when it came to meeting with my friends.

As I backed out of my circular driveway, I looked at my two-story, brick-faced, four-bedroom home. It was part of the settlement I received in my divorce. It was a lot of space for a single woman. Sometimes the house echoed with loneliness, but at other times, it didn't seem big enough for all the shit I put up with during my marriage. I shook my head as I reminisced on some of the hurtful things that man put me through but decided I better try to refocus my thoughts as I took in the sun and the beautiful green trees that the spring day provided.

"Well, look at you!" Fallon said as she got up to hug me. "I'm loving those braids, bae. You look great!" Fallon was always one to offer up a compliment. I looked at Fallon—flawless as usual. Her creamy, tan skin was in contrast to her crimson, reddish-brown hair. She always wore a matte reddish-brown lipstick that complimented her hair and skin nicely. Fallon was short in stature and voluptuous. She oozed perfection as she was always very neat and well put together.

"You smell great! What scent is that?" I asked as I took her in.

"It's a new one from my spring line of fragranced body oils called Pure. I was hoping you would like it, girl," Fallon said as she patted my hand before handing me a small gift bag full of goodies.

"Girl, thank you! You know I love all your shit," I teased.

We were frequent guests of the downtown Atlanta establishment, so we didn't even pick up the menu. When the waiter came over, we ordered our food and drinks and waited for him to leave before we began our chitchat.

"So how you been?" I asked Fallon. I knew she kept busy with her business, but I wanted to know if she had anything new brewing on the romantic side. I was hesitant to tell her about my sexcapade, but I rarely kept anything from my girls.

"I've been good. No complaints, just trying to keep up with the rest of all these lines out here. You know everybody *organic* and reinventing the wheel with the same shit over and over." Fallon was really expressive when she spoke, and she formed quotation marks with her hands as she emphasized organic.

"I feel you. Well, I tell everybody about your line whenever I can," I boasted.

"I know you do, girl. Nothing like support from your team. So what have you been up to? I see Wyn doing her thing with

Khalil. Who would've ever thought Wynter would get caught up?" Fallon said as she shook her head.

"I haven't been up to much except eating my way through life." I joked.

"You look good, sis. You know the thicker the better 'round here."

We talked through dinner, laughing heartily as we always did when we were together. Just as I was dabbing the corners of my mouth I spotted them at a table on the far end of the restaurant behind Fallon. I tried to avert my eyes hoping that if we avoided eye contact, I could make it out of there without them seeing me.

"Are you okay?" I heard Fallon ask, snapping me out of my thoughts.

"What?" I stuttered.

"You good, girl? You looked wide eyed for a second there." Fallon turned around and looked behind herself, scanning the tables for the source of my attention.

"Don't look." I admonished.

"Don't look at what?" Fallon was clueless.

Just then, I saw them get up and walk toward my table. I felt my heart beating in my chest and between my thighs.

Kris and her commanding ass walk reached our table first with O trailing closely behind her. "Spree! It's so good to see you again." She looked at Fallon as if she were waiting for me to make an introduction.

"Fallon, this is Kris and Omari. I met them a few weeks ago. Funny… It was at dinner. I guess we all really like to eat out." I joked, then realized it was a Freudian slip.

"Don't we?" Kris was snarky.

It felt weird. Kris standing there like a jealous lover who caught me cheating on her. I broke the second-long silence.

"Okay, it was nice seeing you both again. We must keep in touch." I hoped that was enough to send them on their way. Omari picked up my hand and placed a gentle kiss on it.

"Don't be a stranger, Spree," he said as he placed his hand on the small of Kris's back and ushered her away.

"What the fuck was that about?" Fallon questioned.

"Girl. I don't even know. I met them a few weeks ago at a hotel bar after one of my nightmare dates. They invited me to join them for dinner. I was bored, so I did. They're a cool couple," I offered as I swallowed the rest of my drink down in one gulp. In my mind, I was annoyed. They hadn't reached out to me since that night—not a single word, but now they want to stand in front of me like old lovers? *Fuck outta here.* I thought that. I really did, but my body was having a different reaction. My panties were soaked through as I imagined O's meaty stick in his hands and in me while Kris had her mouth on my breasts as I played with her kitty.

The next day, after spending more than I should on new clothes that were a match for my recent weight gain, I shuffled in my house with my arms full. I really didn't need more clothing, but shopping always took my mind off of things. I heard my phone buzzing, so when I put my bags down, I reached for my phone to see who was texting me.

O: I never got to say thank you for the evening you spent with us. Seeing you again the other evening was a good reminder. I'd love to have you over for brunch on Sunday. Say you'll come.

I read it and then read it again. "I should just delete this shit," I mumbled to myself. Instead, I replied, *OK.*

I didn't have a clear answer as to why I was agreeing to meet up with him again. *Is Kris going to be there?* I wondered. Omari sent me the address to his or their place. I wasn't sure if they lived together or not since they were engaged. I felt a wave of butterflies moving throughout my stomach. I went through my bags of new clothes, putting together the perfect outfit for Sunday brunch. O's address was in Buckhead—my old town. When I was married, we had a mansion in Buckhead, but after his mistress came to our house with her belly, I threw in the towel and had him buy me a mini mansion across town in Dunwoody.

Sunday morning, I woke up full of anxiety thinking I should cancel and not go to Omari's. What was I really getting myself into if I did go? I put my Keurig on and made myself a cup of espresso. I walked out onto my back patio and sipped my espresso as I scrolled through Instagram. Everyone seemed to be so happy, living their lives, and living in the moment, and although I knew that people only post their best moments, I wondered when I would be able to post mine. I had been basically single since my divorce. A few short-term friends with benefits situations, but nothing substantial. I sat back listening to the birds chirping on the beautiful spring day and had an epiphany. Perhaps I've been looking at relationships the wrong way. Kris and Omari were both beautiful, successful, and seemed to be in love, but they invited me into their bedroom. My ex used to tell me that sex and love were two separate things, but I couldn't get over the fact that if a man loved you, they would still desire other women. I was sure Omari loved Kris, but that didn't stop him from enjoying me.

I entered the beautiful gated community in Buckhead. It was nostalgic as I passed some of my old stomping grounds. Buckhead held a lot of my happiest and saddest moments, yet I was hoping today would be the former. I drove into the circular driveway and parked my late-model, cream-colored Audi. I took a deep breath before ringing the bell.

"Here you go, girl," I said to myself low enough so only I could here.

"Just when I thought you couldn't look any more beautiful," O's deep baritone said as he stepped back before pecking me on the lips. I was taken aback by the kiss but accepted it as I blushed. He continued his compliments.

"Yellow is your color. Spin around for me."

I did a twirl as my floor-length, strapless chiffon sundress lifted, sending a nice breeze up my thighs. I needed the cooldown.

"You have a lovely place," I said as I stepped in, admiring the black, white, and red modern decor.

From the black-and-white marble floors to the black leather sectional with the red throw pillows, Omari's place was without a lot of fuss. Bright, white walls were covered with black-framed portraits from what looked to be like movies and shows he worked on. I was impressed. I could also see that his place was very much a bachelor's pad. I didn't get the sense that a woman lived there.

"Does Kris live here as? Will she be joining us?" I asked, unsure if I wanted her to join us or not.

"No. Kris has her own condo in Downtown Atlanta. She prefers the busy. I don't know if she's ready for life in suburbia just yet." Omari chuckled to himself.

"Oh. I don't know why I thought with you guys being engaged—" I cut myself off before I sounded too old fashioned.

"We've been engaged for three years. I don't know if we'll ever move past that. It's nice to be engaged, especially for women." Omari smirked.

"You're funny." I poked at him. "That is a long engagement, but if it ain't broke…" I chided.

"Exactly. I'm happy you came today. Come on, I have a spread for you waiting in my sunroom. I hope you're hungry." O said as he guided me to his sunroom.

I was excited by the spread he had laid out. I'm a foodie, and my mouth watered at the sight. A pan of well-done pork bacon, a pan of turkey bacon, beef sausage, golden-brown pancakes sitting on a warmer, redskin potato home fries, a pan of scrambled eggs with shredded cheese on the side, bagels with cream cheese, Dom

Perignon and orange juice, whipped cream, and strawberries sat before me. I felt like a pig who was about to roll in some slop.

"Now before you go lamenting the compliments, I got this catered. This spread did not come from these paws," he said as he held up his hands.

"Well, it looks great nonetheless," I offered.

We sat down and ate like we hadn't had a meal in a long time. Everything was delicious. I was glad I wore a dress so that I didn't have to unbutton my pants.

"This was so good. Thank you for inviting me."

"I'm glad you came. I wanted to get a chance to spend a little time with you. Alone. I hope you don't mind," He said coyly.

"I don't. But I also don't want to cause any friction with you and yours. Kris is cool, and as a woman who's been hurt, I'm not trying to be the one dishing it out."

Before I could say another word, Omari smeared some whipped cream on my lips and licked it off. I was frozen for a second before I came to and sucked his tongue, enjoying the taste of the cream.

Omari leaned into me from his seat, never removing his lips from me. He slid his hand up my dress and rubbed my thigh before grabbing a handful of the fleshy thickness of my thigh and moaned. I felt self-conscious as I quickly compared my thick thighs to the slender, modelish thighs of Kris. As O's hand roamed the length of my thigh reaching at the highest place where my hip met my thigh, I let out a light gasp. Omari stopped and stood me up. He knelt down in front of me and lifted my dress and put it over his head.

I felt his tongue as he licked from just above my knee and around to my inner thigh. I felt the lightest prick of teeth as Omari grabbed a hold of the string of my thong from my right hip and began to tug my panties down. With his teeth, he eased them down my thighs and over my knees. I stared at the ceiling, admiring the etched in crystal-like pattern that was blended into his white paint. I stepped out of my panties, and Omari forcefully parted my legs from under my dress. I stood there in his sunroom, and as his tongue parted my lips and pressed against my flesh, I let my head fall back, relishing in the power of his tongue. I could hear him lapping my juices like a dog who got to drink after a long run.

I pulled my dress from over his head and pulled it over my head and tossed it on the lounge chair. Omari took my hand and led me up the stairs to a room I'm imagining is his bedroom. He sat me down on a chaise lounge and prompted me to lay back. I didn't ask any questions; I laid back. Omari took my left leg and draped it over the side of the chaise, leaving me exposed, open, and wide for his eyes to see. I watched him as he stood there for a few moments taking me all in. He rubbed his hand over his goatee.

"You look so good... You taste so good. Can I have some more?" I knew it wasn't really a question he was waiting for an answer for.

Omari dropped to his knees again and devoured me. I was having mini convulsions on his chaise lounge—the same lounge I was sure Kris's ass had been spread open on. O paused on the meal in front of him with his eyes low.

"Damn, guh, your pussy pretty," he said with lust increasing his southern drawl.

I arched my back and opened my legs wider, ensuring he was able to fully view my pretty pussy that was waiting for him for his tongue to return. Omari backed up and walked away while licking his lips.

"I gotta get inside you."

I propped myself up on my elbows watching him as he returned with a condom. He had it between his teeth as he opened the package and guided it over his thick shaft. I couldn't help but lick my lips at the sight of his thickness and in anticipation of what I was about to feel.

"On your knees," he demanded as he pulled me up aggressively.

I got on my knees on the chaise and scooted my round ass up, making sure the arch in my back was deep. Omari spread my ass cheeks apart and entered my wet opening slowly. He began to pump with his flat abs hitting my ass as my cheeks bounced to the rhythm we were creating. I groaned as Omari grabbed a handful of my long braids and wrapped them around his hands. He used my braids like he was on a horse holding the reins. I bucked back, taking him in as deep as my canal would allow, squeezing his dick tight with my pussy contracting with every thrust.

"Damn this shit is good," he mumbled.

"Fuck me, Omari. Harder!" I moaned.

Before I ran into Omari and Kris, I had been in a sexual drought. I intended to enjoy all the orgasms I could get while I could.

Omari fucked me like he had something to prove. I think my asking him to fuck me harder was motivation for him to go deeper. I could feel the moisture dripping on my back as sweat dripped from his forehead. O pulled my hair, and then I felt the sting from the slap on my right ass cheek.

"This juicy ass can take all this dick," Omari said through what sounded like clenched teeth.

"Damn sho," I said as I bucked back wildly, determined to finish us both off with explosive orgasms.

"Ughhhh. Arghhhh. Shit!" he moaned as he leaned in close over me. His body shuddered against my back.

"Ohhhh, u-ughhhh," I stuttered as the sounds of release vibrated off of his walls. I didn't want to get used to dick that didn't belong to me. Then again, what dick really belonged to any one woman? They were all just loaners for the time being as they usually were being lent out and shared with others at some point.

The heat from my hot tub was exactly what my throbbing vagina needed. I poured some more lavender-scented Epsom salt from Fallon's spa line in and leaned my head back. I was having flashbacks of the welcomed assault Omari placed on my lady parts. We had been spending time together eating, drinking, sexing, and texting for weeks. I sipped my favorite coconut wine and smiled to myself. I picked up my remote and turned on the flat screen that sat on the wall opposite my tub. I searched for the television show that Kris starred in and pulled it up on demand. She was a fair actress. Her beauty outweighed her acting skills, but who was I to judge? I watched her and thought about how it felt to have her tongue flickering against my slit. I also wondered why, with all her beauty, she wasn't enough to fill Omari's big sexual appetite. I outweighed her by a full thirty pounds. I guess he had a taste for variety.

As I'm drying off, I heard my phone buzzing. I pick it up expecting a group message from Wynter, Summer, or Fallon, but I'm surprised when I see it's from Kris. I panic for a quick second, wondering if she knows and is upset about my visit to Omari's place.

K: Hey. It feels like forever since dinner. Are you free on Sat?

I breathed a sigh of relief. I wasn't sure what they had going on in terms of their relationship, but I didn't want to cause any waves, despite the fact that after that dick down, I knew I would have a hard time stopping.

Me: I was actually just thinking about you. Saturday I'm free. What do you have in mind?

I wasn't lying. I had just been thinking of her as I watched her show.

K: Cast party at Havana. I would love to have you as my guest.

I sighed. I had been to many industry parties. I knew the Atlanta celebrity scene well. From music to movies, I had done all the parties. The phony smiles… the "I'm doing better than you and I'm I doing your man" looks… I wasn't impressed. At the same time, I wasn't doing much else. My closest friends seemed to be caught up in their own lives, so why not? It was something to do. Besides, it would give me a chance to see Omari again.

It took me an entire day to take my braids out so that I could get my hair done in preparation for Saturday night's event. I had the finest Brazilian body wave attached to my head and the cleanest Brazilian between my legs. I stepped into my black, strapless, sequin mini dress and turned for Summer to zip me up.

"Wow, missy, you look like er'thang!" Summer said as she snapped her fingers and faked a southern accent.

"Guh! I didn't eat for a week so that I could get into this shit." I turned around, admiring my ass in my floor-length mirror.

"You in it, bitch! You wearing that shit. Who did your hair? Shit look like it's growing from your scalp." Summer admired.

"Kira, down on Ponce. This hair was hella expensive, but it feels like silk," I said as I pulled my fingers through the jet-black hair.

"Let me get out of here and let you finished getting dressed. I just wanted to stop by and shoot the breeze with you before I head to Tori's. We've all been so busy these days. I miss y'all," Summer whined.

"I'm glad you did. I have so much to catch y'all up on. How are things with Tori?"

"I bet you do. You can start with telling me now." Summer prodded. "And Tori... He's okay I guess," she added.

"He's just okay? I guess we all need to sit down and chat," I stated as I watched Summer, looking for a hint of unhappy. She seemed like she was lost in thought.

"Yes, just okay. I don't know, Spree. I've been thinking about Dre a whole lot lately. What I have with Tori is cool, but what I had with Dre was supernatural. Our vibe was just different," Summer explained.

"No, I get it. That feeling doesn't just come along with anyone. You ever think about reaching out to Dre? I'm sure he would be happy to hear from you," I said as I applied a new stick of Mented Cosmetics Red Carpet lipstick.

"I doubt it. Listen, let me get out of here so you can go show your ass at that party. You look so hot," Summer said as she took my black patent-leather, Christian Louboutin four-inch heels from the shelf in my shoe closet and handed them to me.

"Okay. This conversation is to be continued. I'll call you tomorrow," I said. Summer was like my little sister. As hard as it was to find, be, and stay in love, I didn't want her to end up with Tori just because she settled.

"Sounds like a plan. Love you, sis. We'll catch up tomorrow. I'll see myself out." Summer pecked me on the cheek and went on her way.

I walked into the sexy club and checked my phone to see if Kris had messaged me. Just as I was about to look up, I smelled her and then felt the heat from her breath on my neck.

"I was hoping you would show. You look sexy as always," Kris whispered seductively in my ear.

I smiled at her compliment and turned to face her. Kris was never one to be outdone. She had on a red, short romper that barely covered her mini cakes. Her breasts sat high, and the deep V-cut neckline plunged down to her taut navel. Her see-through, five-inch heels gave her a few inches over me. She had her black hair slicked back in a sleek neck-length bob. We sized each other up as our ice breaker.

"You look great as always. I love that romper. Hermes?" I questioned, admiring the design.

"Givenchy, baby," Kris boasted.

Kris grabbed my hand before I could say another word.

"Come, I want you to meet some of the cast. They're like family," she said as she led the way to a table in the VIP section of the club.

"Everyone this is my guest, Spree. Spree, this is my team." She gushed.

"It's very nice to meet you all. You're all very talented. You have a fan in me." I lied. I really wasn't a fan of the evening soap-like drama, but I was happy to be in Kris's company.

"I see you've met everyone." I heard his baritone over from over my shoulder.

Watching Omari walk over in a black button-up shirt, black blazer, and black slacks turned me on. He had this way about him that seemed to get everyone's attention when he spoke. He was fine. I smiled, but not too hard. I didn't want to give off the energy that I was happier to see Kris's man than she was.

As he eyed me from head to toe, I wanted to turn, bend, twerk a bit, stick my tongue out, and kick my leg up. But I just smirked, knowing that he liked what he saw. Hearing Kris's voice made me remember that she was there, and perhaps I better stop drooling.

"Here, girl. Drink up," Kris said as she handed me one of the pretty pink drinks the server had just brought to the table.

"I'd like to make a toast," Kris said as she raised her glass. The rest of the cast of pretty people at the table raised their glasses on her command.

"To new friends, love, life, and our futures. May success and lots of sex be showered on us all!" Everyone laughed heartily. Her toast seemed to be an agreeable sentiment of everyone.

I downed my drink as I watched Kris whisper in Omari's ear before leading him to the dancefloor. I watched them dance. Kris grinded her hips to the beat, pulling Omari's face to hers, and she kissed him passionately. I felt a twang of jealousy and a bit of loneliness. Before I could cover myself in self-pity, a nice-looking guy, who appeared to be several years younger than me, came over to me.

"Why is such a beautiful, sexy woman standing over here alone? You need to let me get you out on that dancefloor," he said.

I took him in. He had caramel, smooth skin, light mustache, thick eyebrows, and low waves. He smelled good too. I picked up another drink as the server passed by and drank it quickly before responding.

"Okay. Let's go fuck it up." I pumped my pelvis and led him onto the middle of the floor.

I could see Omari and Kris taking turns watching me. It was like one would stop watching, and then the other would begin their staring shift. I made sure I gave them something to see as I let the young buck have his way with me as much as one could while dancing. I threw my head back in an exaggerated laugh as he whispered bullshit in my ear. I really couldn't hear it well over the music, but I laughed heartily as if whatever he was saying was more than worth hearing.

"Can I cut in?" It sounded like more of a demand then a question. I looked at Kris as she stepped in between my young dance partner and me.

Kris put her hands on either side of my hips and danced closely to me. I wasn't sure how I should react. I was concerned that her castmates were watching and may be able to pick up on the sexual energy between us. Then I thought about it and figured if she didn't care, why should I? I turned around so that my back was to her and pushed my ass against her groin as we swayed to the beat.

"How was brunch?" I heard her whisper from behind me.

I wanted to freeze. I wasn't sure how I should respond. But I guess she already knew. I turned around to face her. I didn't want to seem like I was hiding anything.

"Brunch was great. I was surprised you weren't there," I said in her ear over the music. Kris looped her arm in mine and walked me off the dancefloor. She took a seat at the bar and pulled out a chair for me.

"Bartender, we'll have two of the house specials." She smiled as she placed the order. Then she turned to me. Her smile had disappeared.

"Listen, Spree, if you're going to fuck my man, you best believe I'm gone know." The friendly demeanor she possessed earlier no longer existed.

Her smile returned as the bartender placed our drinks in front of us. I was taken aback but one never to be made a fool out of. I knew I had to put her back in her place.

"Am I sensing anger? I thought you would be okay with it. You were okay with sharing his dick with me a few weeks ago. Or is it only okay if you get to eat my pussy before he sticks his dick in it?" I raised my eyebrow and sipped my drink.

Kris' smirked. "That may be. I like eating your pussy, and it seems you like it to be ate. I hope you don't think you're the first one to join us in the bedroom," she said sarcastically.

"No. That wasn't ever my assumption. I see how you two get down, and while this is my first experience like this, I've been around the block. My question to you is why are you coming at me like this if I'm just another fuck for you two? You're his fiancée, and you have the ring," I said as I held up her left hand.

"True indeed. I do have his ring, and right now, I have his heart as well. I want to keep it that way. His dick… Well, it's just an extension of him. Dicks roam—it's what they do. But his love, his heart, his affection… those belong to me. I just wanted to make myself clear," Kris said as she snatched her hand away.

I scoffed. Apparently she sensed something between Omari and I that I wasn't even aware of. I knew I was attracted to him and that I actually enjoyed his company, but I didn't know the feeling may have been mutual until that moment.

"Thanks for the drink," I said as I got up and left Kris sitting there, ending our conversation, whether she was finished or not.

On that note, I figured it was time for me to go so I made my way to the VIP ladies' room to relieve my bladder before I took the ride home. I was washing my hands when I heard the door open and lock. When I looked up, I almost jumped. Omari's reflection staring at me as he stood silently caused my heartrate to speed up.

"You… You… I don't know, but there's something about you that I can't get enough of," he said. His usual deep voice was now raspy and sexy.

I turned my back to the sink and took him in. I bit my lip. His chocolate skin was so smooth and flawless. I wanted to lick him.

"I think I better be going. I don't know what this is, but it doesn't feel right," I said as I tried to walk past him.

"It doesn't feel right? You a lie. Everything about this feels right," he said as he took my face in his hands and kissed my lips like he was mine, knowing I was his.

Omari backed me up to the sink, lifting me up on it. He didn't have to open my legs; I spread them widely. His tongue roamed my neck as he pulled out my breasts and sucked them abrasively. His breathing was heavy, and he was rough in his handling of me. He dropped to his knees and reached between my legs, and in one snatch, my panties were strewn aside.

"Give me my pussy. I need to taste my pussy," he said breathlessly as his tongue plunged in my hole. He sucked my clit, moving his tongue about until I shuddered. I held his head in place until the last of my orgasmic waves came to shore.

"My shit about to bust through my pants. I need this pussy," he demanded.

O undid his belt and unzipped his pants, and everything fell to his ankles. He grabbed the thick slab of meat between his thighs and pushed himself in. My walls conformed to tightly snuggle the extension of himself. He took one hand and held me around my throat, not hard enough for me to pass out but strong enough to fuck me like he had a point to prove. He fucked me ferociously, and my pussy poured as I came again. Omari moved carelessly, as if we weren't in the bathroom of a club full of people, including his eventual wife. I heard his breaths quickening, and just as he grunted, he pulled his dick out. His warm cum squirted up and landed on my breasts and chin. When he finished his spurt, he folded his dick up and put it back in his pants. Omari pulled me off the sink and pulled my short dress down from around my waist. He dampened a paper towel and wiped me off, cleaning me of his juices. We both washed our hands and exited the bathroom. He returned to the waiting party, and I to my car and my home.

What I intended to leave as a one-night stand had turned into a full-fledged affair. I wasn't sure if I was having an affair, since I was not in a relationship, or if I was the cause of one. I had definitely found my ecstasy. I just hadn't ever planned on it being a he, she, and me kind of situationship. The sound of my doorbell snapped me out of my thoughts. I wasn't expecting any guests, so I figured it was some neighborhood kids selling something as usual.

I opened the door to the biggest bouquet of multicolored roses I had ever seen.

"Delivery for a Miss Spree Samsun," the young, blonde man said.

"What a surprise. Thank you," I said as I took the flowers from him.

"Somebody loves you," he said as he tilted his uniform hat and walked away.

I sat the large vase down on the table in my foyer and eagerly opened the card.

Spree, what an unexpected flower you've been. Blooming in my heart and mind. Looking forward to laying my eyes on you again soon. -O

My heart pounded in my chest. What the fuck am I going to do? He's literally somebody else's guy, so where does my third piece fit in a puzzle that's made for two? I smelled the roses. They were so fresh. It was then that I decided to try not to think about anything else besides the feeling I got when I was in his company. I would take it one day at a time. This new thing I was experiencing, being in a threesome that lasts outside of the bedroom, was unconventional by most standards, but I was feeling happier and wetter than I had in a long time, and that meant more than anything.

Summer

"If you stay stuck in the past season or fixated on the future season,

you will miss the one you're in." -Maree Dee

"I can't believe this shit! She really married and had kids with that mothafucka!" I heard Tori mumble out loud.

"Who married who?" I asked as I entered his sunken den with a bowl of cherries. We had just finished round two of a session of afternoon lovemaking. I thought Tori had dozed off, but he was lying on the couch, looking at his phone closely.

"That damn Sasha had kids with that white guy she married... this Bryan dude she used to work with."

I rolled my eyes before putting my bowl down. I cocked my head to the side, making sure I heard him clearly.

"Sasha? As in your old girlfriend Sasha?"

"Yeah, her. I can't believe this." Tori shook his head.

"Let me ask you a question, Tori. Why are you even worried about who Sasha married and had kids with? Didn't you guys break up years ago, and how the hell do you know what's going on in her life anyway?" My annoyance was fully displayed.

Tori stuttered as he sat up on the couch to cover himself.

"I-I-I just happened to be on Facebook, and she came up as a suggested friend. Her page is open, so I just started looking around, and I saw that she just had her second kid. I felt a way because dude was supposedly just her friend when we were engaged, and now he's her husband. Shit don't sound foul to you?" Tori asked.

"No, it don't sound foul to me. But what does sound foul is the fact that you just got out of me, and you're playing op, searching through your ex's page. I don't know how you think I'm supposed to feel about that, but that's what foul to me."

I snatched my shirtdress that had been thrown, landing on his desk in a moment of passion not much earlier and pulled it over my head in a huff.

Tori looked at me bewildered. "Where do you think you're going?"

"I'm gonna leave you to your vices. You want to sit and cyber stalk Sasha a few minutes after you finish fucking me? Nah, I'm gonna give you all the time you need to get through all her and her family pics. Call me when you're finished. As a matter of fact, don't call me!"

I slipped on my slides and started making my way to the door of his townhouse with him close on my heels.

I got to the door, and as I opened it, he slammed it closed, blocking me from leaving.

"You being fucking crazy, Summer. Don't leave because I'm looking at pictures. Come on now. It's me and you."

I swiped his arm down from the door, and proceeded to open it with a shoulder shove of him out my way. I stopped before I got completely out of the door.

"I'm not leaving because you looked at pictures. I'm leaving because she still has an effect on you. I'm leaving because you felt compelled to look at her pictures. But I get it. Trust me. I do."

I smirked and stomped out to my car.

As I drove to my apartment, I couldn't help but feel a little guilty for getting upset with Tori. You see I totally understood what he was going through. When you miss out on living life with the one, you don't just get over it. You don't just move completely on. You never do. I had been Facebook stalking my ex, Dre, for over a year. I created a fake business page like I was a company that supplied laundromat cleaning supplies just to watch him. I watched him on Instagram too living his life. I missed him and knew I would never love another man like I loved him again, so I would just settle with watching him from afar.

Tori I have love for, but it's nothing like what I had with Dre, and I can tell I'm no Sasha. Tori's successful, smart, handsome, and a decent lover. But he's no Dre. He doesn't get my fire started with just a look, smile, or simple touch. I left Dre behind in New York, but I could've and should've done better. He deserved more than a last roll in the sack and "Dear John" letter. But at the time, I didn't know how else to handle my chickens that had come home to roost.

I was, for lack of a better word, a high-paid hoe. I was a madam running my own lucrative escort business in New York City. I demanded top dollar for my girls and even more for the honey pot that sat between my thighs. When you understand the art of seduction, it's not hard to get a man's last dime. He wants the euphoric experience of a nut from his fantasy woman, which is only something money can pay for. I took full advantage of men's weaknesses and turned it into my fortune. Unfortunately, I had business partners who weren't as smart as I was when it came to clientele, and you know what they say about sleeping dogs. Yeah, I woke up with some fleas. In the course of operating my business, I was a full-time student, and it was in school that I met the bright, intelligent, gorgeous Dre. I fell in love with him when I didn't think I would ever love anyone. He showed me a side of men that I didn't think existed and something so pure I didn't think I was worthy of. At the time, I wasn't.

So here I am, involved with Tori, who's still as in love with his ex as I am with mine. Tori talked about building a life with me, and I've thought about building a future with him. But it's not because we're just so into each other; it's more because we fit. I look great on his arm, and I fit in with the other trophy wives his fellow attorneys have at home. For me, Tori is successful, so I know I'll always have a substantial bank account, so he fits in the ways that I need him to. Outside of that, he's a nice-enough guy and a decent-enough lover. In my former line of business, I've certainly had worse.

After showering and running some shampoo and water over my fresh, blonde buzz cut, I sat on my balcony overlooking Atlanta while sipping a glass of chilled Chardonnay. I checked my emails, sent a few texts to my sister-friends, and finally allowed myself to do what I had been wanting to do since I got home. Tori's mishap gave me a lot to think about, and recent conversations with my friends had put things in perspective. I clicked on Dre's page, and the first thing that popped up caused my heart to beat quickly. It was a picture of him with a girl... Well, a woman. They were both smiling broadly, and he had his hand over her shoulder. Not exactly lovey-dovey, but hell, he was touching her, and that was more than enough for me. He hadn't posted pictures with any female after me. He and this chick had just checked in at a hotel in Laurinburg, North Carolina.

I stood up and paced my small balcony. I wondered what he was doing in North Carolina and with this chick no less. I zoomed in on her face, and she was cute, brown skinned and had pretty dimples, nice teeth, and her hair slicked up in a high bun. I plopped back down and rolled my eyes at the screen. I didn't understand why I was so upset. Of course, he needed to move on. I did... if you call my superficial relationship with Tori "moving on". I clicked on message and decided to do what I had been debating with myself about doing for the last year. I started my message.

Me: Hey, Dre. It's me, Summer, not BP Laundry Supplies. LOL.

Then I realized how stupid that sounded, so I erased it. I put my phone down and turned on Netflix. I queued up Titanic and sobbed as Jack drifted off the glacier of ice. The movie had me imagining that Jack was Dre, and I was Rose, left to spend the rest of my life without the man of my dreams. I cringed, thinking about how much time I had already lost with Dre, so I decided to message him, even if it means I get embarrassed by his rejection. My last email to him was so final. I'm sure he's feeling a way about how I ended things.

I took a deep breath and began.

Hi, Dre. It's me, Summer. You may not want to hear from me. I understand if you don't, but I felt I needed to reach out to you. I guess the first thing I should be saying is that I'm sorry. Sorry for leaving you in any pain and with unanswered questions. I have known for a while that perhaps I could've handled things differently. Don't ask me why I'm under BP Supplies. I felt it would be a way for me to somehow stay connected to you even from a distance. As for me, I'm well. Things have been going good, both personally and professionally. I hope things are well on your end, although I must say you look like you haven't missed a beat. My gorgeous guy, LOL. I don't expect to hear from you. I'm satisfied with just having reached out to you.

-Your Summer

I clicked off his Facebook page, feeling relieved and anxious simultaneously. I looked at my messages and saw that Tori had been blowing up my phone. I was going to let him sweat a while longer but decided to respond since I really was no better than him when it came to my ex.

I responded with a command, knowing I had him in the palm of my hand.

Me: *I'm hungry. I'll be ready in twenty minutes. Be here.*

I pressed send and decided to find something to wear quickly. I intended on having an expensive meal. It was the least he could do.

Two weeks had passed, and I had put my message to Dre out of my mind, or at least I tried to move it to the back of it. I was lying across my couch naked from the waist down with Tori on his knees consuming me. Tori hated when I smoked, but it was something about smoking a blunt while he ate me out that just made his tongue action that much better. I took a deep pull and blew the haze of smoke out slowly. The fog created a halo over his head that was bowed in my lap. I looked down at his head bobbing up and down and smirked. My high helped me reach a euphoria that his mouth couldn't. Just as I was pulling in some more of the fine greenery, I heard my phone buzz. It was the Facebook alert. Distinct. For once, I was hoping it was coming from my bogus account and not the one linked to my blog. My low eyes instantly widened in anticipation. I put my blunt down and reached for my phone. My movement caused Tori to pause and look up at me. He raised his eyebrows quizzically before he spoke.

"You good?"

"Yeah. I'm good. Keep going. I was almost there. More pressure on my clit," I said as I reached for my phone.

"You really gon' look at your phone while I eat your pussy, Summer? It can't wait?"

"It can't wait. Keep going." I nudged his head between my thighs and lay back with my heart beating rapidly.

I may have looked cool on the outside, but I was trembling on the inside. The weed I just smoked wasn't even enough to calm my nerves. What if it wasn't Dre? What if it was, and he cursed me the fuck out? What if it was just a message with someone sending me a tip on some hot celebrity gossip to post—a scorned side chick, a gay lover of a supposedly straight man? I closed my eyes and took a deep breath before I opened the app.

My heart pounded as I looked at the account the message came from. It was him! He responded!

Damn, Summer. I have had this convo with you a million times in my head, and although it took me awhile, I eventually got over you. I knew you had moved to Atlanta. The internet really doesn't allow anyone to disappear completely. I'm happy to know that you're good otherwise, but I knew that too. What made you contact me all of a sudden? Never mind, don't answer that. Be well. -Dre

Tears welled in my eyes. I was numb. I couldn't even feel what Tori was doing to me. I closed my legs and sat up, momentarily forgetting that Tori was even down there.

"Yo, what the fuck?" Tori cursed. He was still on his knees with his arms raised in the air and a look of confusion and annoyance on his face.

I was silent for a moment before I answered him. "I'm sorry, Tee. I'm just not in the mood," I mumbled.

"I see. You were in the mood a little while ago. Something on your mind apparently," Tori said as he got up and sat down next to me on the couch.

I relit the blunt I was smoking and took a pull. I needed something to help with all of the mixed emotions I was feeling. I didn't want to think about Dre or about the past. I didn't even want to think about the present.

"If you're in the mood for company, you should probably go. I'm not going to be a good host right now," I said as I blew out a cloud of smoke.

"You been acting real funny lately, Summer. If you want to talk, I need you to speak up. I'm supposed to be your man," Tori said as he beat his chest.

I stared ahead as I spoke. "I get it. You should go."

I didn't even notice Tori when he put on his clothes. I heard my apartment door slam, snapping me out of the deep thought I was in.

Tori didn't contact me for almost a week, and I didn't reach out to him either. I knew that he was pissed, and he had every right to be. He was on his knees trying to bring me to an orgasm, and my mind was elsewhere with someone else. I had been doing fine assuming that Dre still missed me. I don't know why I listened to my friends and reached out to him. Now I was left feeling stupid and dejected.

I walked into the small office that served as headquarters for my entertainment blog with my shades still on. It was a small company, but it was mine. I stuck my hand out to Shannel, my secretary, for my mail and closed my office door. I took my shades off and put my head on my desk. I didn't know what I wanted. I picked up the phone and called Tori's office. I needed to apologize for my behavior and suck up to the man that loved me. Not necessarily the man I loved, but the man that loved me. I wasn't his Sasha, but he treated me good enough for the most part. Besides, I left Dre behind with my old life in New York. Why would I want to bring any of that past into the now?

Because he's the love of your life, dummy, I heard my inner voice say.

It didn't matter that he was the love of my life if that love was only on a one-way street. I waited for Tori's secretary to connect us. I rolled my eyes. I fucking hated apologizing. It was not my strongest suit.

"Hey. I'm sorry for last week," I said as soon as I heard him give a heavy sigh into the phone.

"If you're not going to be able to talk to me about what's going on in your head, I don't know what to tell you, Summer. I know things haven't been perfect with us, but I think we make a great pair. But if you're not sure, well, I need to know," Tori said somberly.

"Let me make it up to you. I'll come over tonight. I'll bring dinner with me, and then you can have the dessert I have waiting. I promise it'll be sweet." I knew that would sway him my way. Tori got off on eating my ass almost as much as he got off on fucking me.

"I'm letting you off easy right now, but best believe, I'm punishing that pussy tonight. I should be home by seven. Don't be late." Tori hung up, not waiting for my response. He was used to getting his way. As an entertainment attorney, he had women at his beck and call and a bunch of men who passed themselves off as friends, but they were just a bunch of hangers-on who would eat the crumbs by way of connections that Tori would feed them.

I pulled out the nip of Hennessy I had in my purse and downed it all in one gulp before ringing the bell. Tori answered the door shirtless in a pair of boxers. His muscular back was still damp from the shower. He pecked me on the lips.

"Ahh, The Optimist! You know the way to my heart, baby." Tori did a slight dance as he took the bag from my arms.

"I knew the gumbo would make you happy. I got some oysters and a nice Sauvignon Blanc. We're set for the night," I said as I headed to the bathroom to freshen up before we ate.

I watched Tori as he ate his food. He devoured the gumbo, sucking the crab meat out of one of the claws as he ranted about a case he was working on for an Atlanta rapper. I had a small portion of gumbo. My appetite had been almost nonexistent since I got Dre's message of rejection. As Tori ate, I tried to imagine the next five years, possibly marriage and a child. It didn't seem like the worst-case scenario. Tori was hardworking and good looking. *I could grow to love him like I loved Dre.* I thought.

Tori settled on the couch and turned on Netflix, relishing in the delicious meal that he had just devoured. I snuggled next to him and turned to nuzzle his neck, taking in the delicious smell of his skin. I placed kisses on his face, taking his bottom lip in and nibbling on it gently. I ran my hand up his bare thigh and stopped when I got to the opening of his boxers. I kissed my way down his neck, pausing on his chest, circling each of his nipples with the tip of my tongue. My tongue traced the space between his abs, and then I was face-to-face with his rock-hard dick that stood up and out of the slit in his boxers.

I gave a tug on both sides of his hips and pulled his boxers down. Tori lifted his ass, giving me the assistance I needed to get them down. He kicked them off and sat back. The veins in his dick pulsated. I looked at him to give him eye contact, but he already had his head back with his eyes closed, anticipating the feeling I was about to give him. I stroked his dick up and down, watching as the precum oozed from the head. I placed my lips around his shaft and took him in to the back of my throat. I opened my throat and took him in further 'til I was at the base of his pelvis.

"Ah… damn… Summer, shit," Tori moaned through gritted teeth.

I moaned with his dick in my mouth as I kept my eyes on him, watching for every flinch and every look of ecstasy. I suckled with more pressure as I used my mouth like a human vacuum. The saliva dripped from the sides of my mouth as I moved up and down his dick faster. Tori began to squirm under the pressure and speed of my mouth. Just as his nuts tightened, I took his dick out of my mouth and licked his nuts before gently sucking them. Tori's breathing became audible as he panted and moaned incoherent words. He ran his hands over my head, probably seeking my once long tresses to run his hands through.

I was over it, and I wanted him to be satisfied so that I could go to sleep without having had him inside of me. I grabbed his dick and gave it a few strokes before I placed my mouth back over it. As I sucked it, I moved my tongue around in a rapid pace, ensuring that my tongue was massaging the backside of his dick's head. I could feel the cum rising from his nuts as the veins in his dick throbbed. His warm cum shot straight to the back of my throat as Tori yelled out in passion.

"Shit! Arrrrgh! Shit!"

He thrashed about as I continued to suck him into a flaccid state. Once his dick was completely limp, I removed him from my mouth and smiled. I got off my knees and went to get a warm cloth from his guest bathroom. In the bathroom I spit out his seed and rinsed my mouth with warm water before wetting the white cloth. I wrung it out, and just as I was about to turn off the light and leave the bathroom, I caught a glimpse of myself in the mirror. I stopped and thought about the look on my face. *This feels like a fucking job. Like you're fucking one of your clients, not like you're fucking your man. You know the difference,* I thought to myself.

I turned off the light and returned to find Tori snoring on the couch. I gently wiped over his dick and woke him up so that we could go rest in his bed. I was feeling relieved that I didn't have to let him inside me tonight, but I knew that his dick would be awake before his mind, and it would be looking for the pussy I had avoided giving the night before.

Things were back on track with Tori and I. I had gotten over any hopes of rekindling the flames that I had with Dre in the past. He made it clear that he was over me, and I had to accept that, especially since I knew I had caused him so much pain. I was just finishing lunch with Spree when I heard my phone's Facebook Messenger alert go off.

"What's wrong?" I heard Spree ask.

I didn't realize that my eyes had grown wide at the sound of the alert.

"My Facebook Messenger alert just went off. Probably just some gossip. I don't message with anyone outside of business, and the other account I don't use except to stalk Dre. Well, I used to stalk Dre." I half smiled.

"Well, didn't you say that was the way you communicated with him? Girl, you better check that message!" Spree chided.

"I'll check it later. I'm not sweating him. He said the shit was in the past, so what he want?"

Spree rolled her eyes.

"You think he should've just welcomed you back with open arms after you just walked out of his life? Sis, I know you're used to men falling at your feet, but if this guy is half the catch you claim he is, then you gone have to expect that he's not going to just jump when you decide to reappear out of nowhere after being ghost for what? Almost two years?" Spree held up two fingers for extra emphasis.

"I realize how long I've been out of his life. I probably should've just stayed gone, but with the potential for things to get more serious with me and Tori, I just thought I should be sure of what I'm getting myself into. Besides, you bitches encouraged me to go after what I wanted!" I joked.

Spree leaned in and placed her dainty hand over mine.

"No doubt about that. You have to go for what's yours. Trust me, I know. I know my situation is different from yours, but the end result is the same. Omari makes me happy. He's giving me just what I was missing, and not only in terms of the dick." Spree smiled coyly.

I unlocked my phone a bit apprehensive. I looked at the read icon on the blue message header and exhaled.

"Summer, I know I was cold in my response to you. But you have good sense. I'm sure you understand where I'm coming from. I spent a lot of sleepless nights thinking of what could've been. You were everything I could've ever dreamed of. I didn't care about your past... As crazy as that shit sounds, I didn't. What you did was not even give me a chance to love you despite your past. You made that decision for me and that shit just ain't fair. You seemed to have moved on with ease. After I read your message, I was ready to rid you of my thoughts for good but how could that happen? You have been a part of my daily thoughts since our first date. I'm still in NC taking care of some business for my mother—who on a side note was

crushed by your sudden disappearance. If you really want to see me,
I'm staying at the Marriott in Laurinburg. My number hasn't
changed. You don't have to send any more messages via Facebook.
I'll be here for another week. If I don't hear from you, know that I
wish you well. Always.

I looked up from my phone and met Spree's eyes.

"He's still in North Carolina, and he's willing to see me."

"Then I guess dinner is over. Get to planning your trip. Go see if the chemistry's still there. If it is, Summer, you better not let him go. If it's not, then you can settle for what you have now, and move the fuck on with your life."

Spree picked up her cocktail and finished what was in her glass before continuing.

"As for me, I'm going to enjoy the rest of my night with the triangle that has now become my love life. Not ideal, but it works," Spree said proudly.

"So you're good with her still being in the picture? I don't know if I could ever be okay with that," I told her. We were usually upfront with each other.

"Summer, you of all people know that in one way, shape, or form, it's always a 'he, she, and me' type of thing going on in any relationship at one point or another. Whether or not it's acknowledged or accepted… Well, that's another thing. I came into their situation. The fact that she's okay with me being a part of their trifecta is something that I'm kind of grateful for. So don't judge me because my situation is not your situation, Wynter's situation, or anyone else's for that matter." Spree admonished.

"I didn't mean to come off as judgmental. I'm the last person who can judge anyone." I lowered my eyes.

"Girl, enough of the self-pity bullshit! Get out of here. Go make your reservations, and get your ass to North Carolina so you can see if it's really still all good with Dre."

I blushed. The thought of seeing Dre had me feeling a high I couldn't even get with the best cannabis I smoked.

We ended our dinner with plans to meet up with the rest of our friends in the next coming weeks. I was so grateful to have friends who were open, honest, and cared enough to give it to me straight. I picked up my phone and texted Dre and told him that I would be in North Carolina by that coming Saturday.

########

I started my drive to North Carolina Friday morning. I didn't plan to see Dre until Saturday, but I wanted to check in to the hotel, get a massage, and relax before our scheduled brunch the next day. Dre made plans to meet at a soul food spot in South Carolina just across the border from North Carolina.

I checked into the same hotel that Dre was staying at with no expectations to see him until Saturday. I was at the counter checking in when I heard his laugh. I suddenly became nervous, wondering if I looked okay. *Should I stay facing front until he passes by? I do have on dark shades, so perhaps he won't even notice me. Maybe he doesn't want to see me just yet. What the fuck do I do?* I thought to myself.

The check-in clerk was finished with our transaction. She gave me a pleasant smile after handing me my key card. When I stood, still facing her, she looked puzzled.

"Is there anything else I can help you with, *ma'am*?" She exaggerated the ma'am part.

Damn it! I had no other choice but to leave the desk now. I tried to think quickly of a reason, but he was close enough that he probably would've recognized my voice anyway. I smiled back at the clerk before taking a deep breath and turning around. My eyes widened, and my heart pounded when I saw Dre standing next to the same chick who was all smiled up with him in the Facebook picture. *No he didn't have me come down here, and his girl is still here too. What kind of shit he into now? 'Cause, I'm not the one,* I thought as I turned my mouth down disappointedly. I didn't think I would feel overwhelmed when I saw him, but I did. Every ounce of love, admiration, and attraction came flooding back. He was so beautiful.

I walked over to the elevator where they were standing and waiting to go to their room when I heard Dre say, "Okay, thank you. You have been so much help! This is going to make the transition so much easier for her. Well for the both of us."

Just as he was finishing his last words, he looked past her and at me. He looked like he saw a ghost.

"Well, if that's all, I'll have you sign the last of the paperwork before you leave town on Sunday. See you then." She brandished a big wide smile as she sauntered past me. Dre stood there frozen, but the emotion behind his eyes told me that his heart still held me deep inside somewhere.

The sound of the elevators ringing letting us know that it was there broke the silent stare between me and Dre

"Summer? What are you doing here? I thought we were meeting tomorrow?" Dre sounded both excited and surprised.

"Well, hello to you too. I decided to check in a day earlier to relax and kind of get myself together before we saw each other, but here we are," I said with a nervous smile.

"You look different. You cut your hair. Let me take your bag. Give me a hug," Dre rambled as he reached for my bag and a hug clumsily at the same time.

As he leaned in for a hug, I inhaled deeply, taking in his scent. It was just how I remembered, so masculine and fresh. I wrapped my arms around his neck and held onto him tightly as if we were the only two in the hotel lobby. Dre held me so tight my feet came up off the ground. When he finally loosened his grip, I reluctantly let go of his neck.

Dre picked up my bag and stepped into the elevator with me trailing behind him.

"What floor are you staying on?"

I had forgotten for a moment what floor the clerk told me, so I pulled out my key card holder to get the floor. "Four."

Dre pressed four, and the doors closed. There was a brief, awkward silence that filled the air as the elevator ascended.

"So what are you doing in North Carolina?" I was curious.

"My mom has decided to sell the business and retire early down here. She's made enough money to have a nice nest egg. So I've been down here helping secure a place for her. She came down a few months ago, found the place, and now I'm doing the closing," Dre said.

"Oh, wow! That's nice. I thought that chick was your new girlfriend at first when I saw the picture of you two on Facebook," I admitted.

Dre chuckled. "Nah. She's just a realtor. That's funny."

We walked to my room in silence, and once I opened my door, Dre handed me my bag.

"You can come in." I held the door open, waiting for him to cross the threshold.

Dre leaned in on my doorjamb. "Nah, I don't think that's a good idea. You get yourself settled in, and if you feel up to it, maybe we can have dinner tonight. Get a head start on our get together."

I felt a bit slighted and confused as to why he would turn down the offer to come inside. I couldn't help but be instantly turned on by seeing him, and I wondered why he wasn't feeling the same way about me.

"Yeah, okay. Dinner then. Text me, and let me know where I should meet you," I said dryly.

"Sure. Okay," Dre said.

I took that as my cue to close the door. Just before the door closed shut, I felt pressure from the other side.

"Sum, I don't think you know how happy I am to lay eyes on you again. I wasn't sure if I would ever have the chance. I'll see you tonight," he said as he let the door go and walked away.

I settled in, showered, and got dressed in preparation for dinner. Dre had texted earlier, saying to meet him down in the lobby at six. I pulled out a white camisole slip top that was framed in lace and a pair of jeans that had rips in the knees and ass. I pursed my lips and applied a ruby-red lipstick. After spritzing myself in all the right places, I slid on my black stilettos and made my way downstairs. When I got to the lobby, Dre was on his phone engrossed in conversation, which he abruptly ended as I approached.

"You look gorgeous as ever. No wonder Amber Rose always looked familiar to me. I couldn't put my finger on it, but seeing you with this short haircut lets me know why now. It looks great on you, but then what wouldn't look great on you, Summer?" Dre licked his lips instinctively.

I blushed. "Thank you. I'm actually letting it grow back out now. I don't know what came over me when I cut it off. I guess I just wanted something different."

"Well, I guess we should be on our way. I hope you're hungry," Dre said as he offered me his arm.

As we sat in his ride, Dre broke the silence that sat between us. The air was thick between us before he spoke.

"You know I thought about just dipping and leaving the hotel after you checked in. Part of me is still pissed at you for how you bounced. Like I really shouldn't even be fucking with you after the way you held your secrets and then left like I didn't deserve an explanation. That shit is crazy." I watched Dre's jaw clench.

"I know. I know, and you have every right to be upset. I think I told you that already. I'm apologizing if I haven't already. I was a few years younger, kinda a lil' black girl lost. I didn't have a mama or father to fall back on, Dre. It was me, out for self. Survival of the fittest. I did what I had to do. I never intended on falling for you. Then when shit hit the fan, I broke out. I didn't want to face you with the side of me that you didn't know. With the side of me that I had deemed unlovable. I just want you to understand that my leaving had nothing to do with my lack of love for you. I haven't ever loved anyone like I love you, and I probably won't ever. I'm just happy you agreed to give me this time," I said.

"I needed this closure, Summer. I couldn't bond with any other woman, knowing you were out there in the world. This closure is good for us both," Dre said as he patted my thigh.

"Closure? Is this what this is?" I asked.

"You're involved with someone aren't you, Summer?" Dre glanced over at me as he drove.

"I am. But—"

Dre cut me off. "Then yes, closure is exactly what this is."

Our table was outside overlooking the water across the border in South Carolina. It was a hot and sticky night, but the breeze coming off the ocean was welcomed. After ordering our food, we both sat looking out at the sun setting over the water. The orange hue was casting a beautiful silhouette over the darkened water. Both silent and lost in our individual thoughts. The sound of my phone ringing broke the peace that the quiet allotted us. I looked down at the screen and sent Tori's call to voicemail. When I looked up, Dre's eyes met mine. Tori called right back, and I sent him to voicemail again.

"You should get that. He may be worried," Dre said as he sipped his beer.

I ignored his comment and took a sip of my red wine.

"You know, Summer, it's not right to up and disappear on a brotha. Did you tell him you were leaving town? I know damn well you didn't tell him you were coming to meet me."

I probably turned a few shades of red. My face felt hot. I didn't come to talk about Tori.

"Are you really concerned about him? I came because I wanted to see you. I knew leaving New York and you behind was probably the biggest mistake of my life."

"So you see me. Do you still think leaving me behind was the biggest mistake of your life? Why now? Why not a year ago?" Dre sat forward, demanding an answer in a passive aggressive way.

"Before I move on to the next phase of my life… the next phase of my relationship with him… I wanted to know if there was still a chance with my heart, my soul mate… with the love of my life." Tears formed in my eyes.

Dre rubbed his hand over his mustache before speaking. "Summer, I have waited for this moment since the morning I woke up to an empty bed. One part of me has been so pissed with you that I regret ever meeting and having the experience of you. The other part of me has been so unfulfilled since you left. It's like a part of my heart has been missing, and who can live without all of their heart?" Dre smirked.

"Do you love this dude?"

"I have love for him. Am I in love with him? No."

"You really think you want to try this again?" Dre asked, pointing to himself.

"If you're willing to do this with me. Dre, I will never let you down. Not ever again." I hoped I sounded convincing.

We took our time eating the fresh grilled lobster and sautéed vegetables. After several glasses of wine, I was feeling light on my feet. As we drove back to the hotel, there was a heat between us in the car. A magnetic force that made me want to sit on his lap as he drove. I needed to feel his touch. My belly was full, but I was starving for his body heat. We got back to our hotel. I hoped he wanted me as much as I wanted him. As he walked me to my room door, I was afraid that he would stay on the other side of the door as he had did earlier in the day. I didn't want pie on my face two times in one day. There was but so much my ego could take.

"So I guess this is where you leave me," I said as I stepped inside my room.

"It is, if that's what you want. If not, then I can come in and let you feel how much I've missed you." Dre leaned in and his juicy lips met mine.

He pushed me back into my room gently with his kiss. His tongue swirled around in my mouth as his hands held my face. I stepped out of my heels without removing my lips from his. He began to place simultaneous kisses and licks on my neck. Dre kissed his way down to the top of my tits as he his hands slid near my hips, lifting my satiny top over my head. He stood back and eyed my big titties, and my nipples were protruding through the lace of my bra.

Dre used his fingers to rub both of my nipples over the lace of my bra. He shook his head and licked his lips as he reached behind me and unhooked my bra. My breasts sprang out, but they sat high. Dre grabbed them both, each hand full and overflowing. He squeezed them before sticking his thick tongue out and licking each nipple. He treated them equally as he took his time sucking one then the other. Dre unbuttoned my pants and pulled them down. As I stepped out of them, Dre stepped back and admired my body. He pulled his crisp, white T-shirt over his head. His body was in tip-top shape. His muscular physique was so sexy. I was so wet anticipating what I knew he was capable of.

Dre led me to the plush chair that sat near the floor-to-ceiling window of our hotel. "Sit down, and lay back," Dre said aggressively. The commanding tone in his voice only made my pussy wetter, and I did as I was told.

Dre kneeled down and parted my legs wide open. He placed his hands around my waist and pulled me down roughly toward the end of the chair. Dre put my legs over his shoulders quickly and put his face in my pussy. I heard him breathe in deeply. He inhaled my scent and looked up at me. "My dick is so fucking hard right now. You don't know what the scent of your pussy does to me. I've missed this," he said in almost a whisper.

Before I could respond, Dre took his tongue and slid it up the slit in my pussy using it to open my lips. He didn't waste time finding the mound of flesh he was looking for as he began to suck and lick my clit. I squirmed under the pressure of his tongue... the tongue that brought me to climax without hesitation. The nerves in between my thighs exploded as the rush of fluid came. I panted, trying to catch my breath. I squealed and moaned as I tried to push his head away. He had already brought me to erupt, but he had no mercy on my now oversensitive clit.

Dre came up for air long enough to pull his pants down. I took advantage of his distraction and pushed him on the floor and helped pull his pants off quickly. His dick sprang straight up as his pants released it from captivity. I held his shoulders down as I mounted his throbbing, thick shaft. As I sat on it, it sank into me inch by inch. I felt relief, and my pussy felt fed. Finally. Dre grabbed my hips and took over, lifting me and his pelvis, pushing my hips down making sure I took every inch of him. As I came up, he pushed in and down. The sounds of me wetness created a weird, sloppy noise that was the theme music to our sexy scene.

"I. Love. This. Dick." Every word interrupted by the force of his dick forcing my canal to widen.

"You sure you miss this dick? I can't tell," Dre said through gritted teeth.

I bounced a little higher. The stroke of my pussy went high enough to cause the tip of his dick to rub against my opening.

"Shit, baby," Dre moaned out loud.

I took that as a sign to show no mercy. I sped up my stroke, bouncing up and down as fast as my pussy would allow. Squeezing my canal as tight as I could, I choked the shit out of his dick. I could see the veins in the side of Dre's caramel neck pulsating as he strained against the nut he was trying to fight off.

"I'm about to cum!"

"So am I!" I moaned as my pussy threatened to betray me. My insides tingled as my body shook. I could feel the heat from Dre's cum mixing with mine. Both of our bodies moved violently as we exchanged the emotions between us through our sex organs. It felt like all that we had both been missing.

We both were breathless as I removed my pussy's grip from him. I was so spent that I lay my head down on his chest and curved my body into his. The smell of his sweat was so soothing, so sweet. Dre turned toward me, holding me close as he could. The last thing I heard before I closed my eyes was the sound of the alert on my phone signaling that I had text messages coming in.

My eyes fluttered open as the glare from the morning sun swept across my lids. The silent alarm never let me sleep. The sound of his heartbeat and the warmth radiating from his chest made for a nice night of sleep. I lifted my head, hoping I wasn't disturbing his rest, only to find him already awake and lost in his own thoughts looking up at the ceiling.

"You're already awake? I don't even remember getting in the bed," I said.

"Yeah. I woke up, and we were both on the floor curled up. I picked you up and tucked you in the bed. I probably should've went to my room then, but I didn't want you to wake up to an empty bed after a night of passion. That just wouldn't be right would it?" Dre propped himself up on his elbows so he could look me in my face. I knew he was being sarcastic. *Was he ever going to let me live that down?*

"If sleeping in your own room would've made you sleep better, then perhaps that's what you should've done." I wasn't going to keep feeling guilty for the mistake I made a few years ago.

"I don't think I would've been more comfortable in my room, Summer."

I got up and moved quickly. My bladder was on full. While in the bathroom, I brushed my teeth, getting out last night's grit. "What do you want me to say, Dre?" I asked, continuing the conversation as I made my way back to the bed.

"I want you to know what you want. I don't want to have to worry about you dipping on me again if shit gets tough. You dipped on your man and came here didn't you? I'm not concerned about dude really, but I need to know what we trying to do here," Dre stated.

"Dre, what about you? We didn't talk much about what you have going on back in New York. I know you getting ass from somewhere. You ready to give whatever you got going on up?" I put the ball back in his court.

Dre chuckled. "Of course I get ass when I need it. I go out with chicks. I am a man. Am I with any one woman? Nah. I don't have nobody to answer to, nobody to go home and cut off. So again, what are we trying to do? If it's just about fucking, then I'm good. I don't need to travel down south for some pussy, even if it's your pussy."

I interrupted him. "That I know. I'm not in love with Tori. I haven't ever been in love with him. You're the only man I have ever really loved. I thought you wouldn't want me once you found out what I had done. But here you are… Here we are. I can't let you or this love go ever again. I love you so much." I leaned in and kissed his beautiful lips.

"That's all I wanted to hear." Dre got up. I watched his dick swing as he made his way to the bathroom. I heard the bath water running, and then he peeked out of the bathroom and held his hand out for me and guided me in.

Check-out time came too quickly. Saturday went by in a blur. We never left my room. Dre ordered room service for breakfast, lunch, and dinner. We skipped our planned brunch and ate each other at every meal. We were exhausted, sweaty, and sticky from the whipped cream that came with our fresh fruit that we had used on each other's bodies. The champagne had us thinking that we could stay in that room in our own little world forever. But the complimentary wake-up call that I had pre-scheduled woke us up from our love-induced slumber and brought us back to the reality that we would have to be apart from each other again. At least for now…

Fallon

I hit the snooze on my alarm, again. I was trying to get back into this dream that had my pussy throbbing and moist. In my dream, I was in the middle of a threesome with two chocolate men with my mouth and nether region full. They were ravaging me completely, and I was just about to cum when my alarm went off. You ever have one of those dreams that feel so real that you want to jump back into them so you can finish?

When I realized that wasn't happening, I turned my alarm off and rolled out of bed. I was scheduled to be on my ex's morning show to talk about a new line of my skin-care products that I'm launching that is focused on treating hyperpigmentation the natural way. I hadn't seen Keith in almost six months, and I was hoping I could make it six years before I ran into his dog ass again, but my publicist said I needed the exposure. It was unfortunate that he happened to have one of the hottest radio morning shows around.

Keith was one of Atlanta's most eligible bachelors. He was very handsome at six feet even with bald head, cocoa skin, neat goatee, and muscular frame. He had a daughter from a previous relationship, close in age to my daughter. The two girls got along like sisters. We had a nice little thing going with me thinking he may even be "the one" until one of his side chicks put him on blast on Instagram. Apparently, he hadn't given her money for some new designer clothes, and she went ballistic. It was very embarrassing as we had a very public relationship, walking red carpets, attending very publicized outings together. So when the story was about to break on the blogs, Summer called me to give me the heads up.

What I thought we had built was a solid foundation was nothing more than some shit built on quicksand. Not only did he cheat on me, but he was out here cheating with young chicks that just saw him as an opportunity to fund their spending habits. Ludicrous to say the least.

I walked into the radio station tense. As I stepped onto the elevator, I looked in the wall-to-ceiling mirror and ran my hand through my shoulder-length, auburn tresses. I took a quick peek over my shoulder at my ass in the brown, fitted pants I had purchased for my appearance, and then I looked down at my feet. The knee-high, open-toed boots exposed my fresh pedicure painted in my signature pumpkin-orange color. I knew he would be checking me out from head to toe. I even left a few extra buttons undone on my button-up shirt, knowing that my ample cleavage was a soft spot for him. I stepped off the elevator and met my publicist, Jackie, at the entrance to the studio.

"Good morning, gorgeous! Now remember, he's the host, not your ex. Okay?" she said.

I rolled my eyes at Jackie before answering her. "Jackie, come on now. I'm a big girl. Matter of fact, I'm a grown ass woman, and this is my business. I'm going to treat him like every other host. We gucci," I said and walked by her and into the studio.

Our eyes met, and I extended my hand. "I'm Fallon," I blurted out.

He shook my hand and introduced himself. "Very nice to meet you, Fallon. I'm Rocky. I'll be producing your segment today." He was still holding onto my hand when Keith walked in.

"Oh, I see you two have become acquainted. Rock, this is the beauty I told you about. The one that got away." Keith chuckled awkwardly.

We let go of each other's hands. I looked at Keith and put on a fake smile. I tried to make it warm.

"Hi, Keith. It's good to see you. Thanks for having me on the show." I tried.

"Listen, I still get thank yous from friends in LA who thank me for putting them on to your line. They were spending all of this money on exclusive European lines when your stuff is better for half the cost."

I smirked. "Yeah, well, that's usually how it goes. I got that quality. Why spend your money on overpriced, over-labeled bullshit? But you know how it goes. Folks think spending more means they're getting better." I cut my eyes and turned my attention back to Rocky.

"Have you been here long?" I inquired, knowing Keith had steam coming out of his ears.

"About six months, but it feels like six years. This place is so busy, and I love it," Rocky admitted.

"Your accent tells me you're not an Atlanta native," I said, ignoring the stare I could feel coming from Keith.

"No. Patterson, New Jersey's home for me."

Keith cleared his throat, breaking our conversation up. "We got a few minutes before showtime, and I need to go over a few things with Rock. We're just about to get started."

I sat down in the place reserved for guests and prepared myself to laugh and joke with Keith for the next hour like we're old friends. Should make for great Instagram posts later.

He must've been a new hire. I hadn't seen him around the station during any of my previous visits. I hoped that he would be inside the studio during the interview. He was a really nice piece of eye candy. He had tar-black skin that glowed and curly, jet-black hair cropped low on the sides and about an inch long on the top, thick, black eyebrows, almond-shaped eyes, a long but nice nose, and thick lips neatly outlined by a well-shaped goatee. His physique told me he spent time working out, but he wasn't so built that he looked silly. Rocky even smelled good. Our brief interaction had me curious.

The segment went well, despite the fact that Keith openly flirted with me. I'm not sure if he did it to throw off the energy between Rocky and I that was palpable in the room full of other people. Rocky eyed me during the segment and smiled when I caught his eye. I gave him the eye in return, letting him know I was interested in whatever he was serving up. During the interview, callers dialed in, giving my products rave reviews. I never thought when I started my skin-care line in my mother's kitchen a decade ago that I would be here today. But here I am, being interviewed on a highly-rated morning show. My business is putting up nice figures. My daughter's in college doing well. I was able to buy my parents a new home. I'm straight, with the exception of a lack of dick in my life.

After the interview, I chatted with my publicist for a few minutes and made my way toward the elevator. Just as the doors were about to close, Rocky jumped on. He stood in front of me without speaking for a second.

"Great interview. I think you may have boosted the show's ratings a few points this morning with your presence." Rocky complimented.

"I don't know about that. But thank you." I blushed.

"You're a great producer. You know how to lay Keith's show out so it flows. It's not over yet is it?" I asked.

"No. We have a few more segments, but I wanted to catch up with you to see if you'd be interested in having dinner with me soon. Maybe even this evening if you don't have a man or plans." His northern style was evident. He got right to it.

I smiled and looked him over again. "I don't have either."

"So dinner?" Rocky said as the elevator doors opened.

"Yes, dinner sounds great."

Rocky handed me his card. "Text me your number, where to pick you up from, and the time that works for you.

I took the card and looked back at Rocky just as the elevator doors closed.

I think I floated to my car. It felt like my feet never hit the ground.

"I have a mothafuckin' date!" I exclaimed into the phone as soon as Wynter answered.

"Hello to you too. Hold up, a date! With who?" Wynter shrieked. She had been on cloud nine since she met Khalil. There was a certain peace to her now that hadn't been there before, and I've known Wynter for almost twenty years.

"Well, his name's Rocky. He works as an executive producer at WKRT."

"Keith's station?" Wynter asked.

"Yes, girl. I met him when I went to the show this morning." I chuckled.

"I know Keith isn't feeling that. I'm surprised he's letting old boy getting any play with you."

"He tried to make sure Rocky knew that I was once his. Good thing he got his own mind. One man's trash…"

"Is another man's treasure!" Wynter finished.

We talked for a little while longer, catching up on our lives. Wynter and Khalil were splitting their time between Atlanta and Jacksonville every week. Things were moving along nicely in their relationship. I was really happy for Wynter. The woman who never believed in love was all covered in it now.

My phone buzzed, and I looked at my text only to read that Rocky was pulling into my driveway now. I slipped in my black five-inch pumps and gave myself the once-over in my floor-length mirror in my foyer before heading out the door. I knew he wanted to come to my door and knock, but I didn't want to feel any pressure to let him in. Besides, if I let him in as backed up as I was, we may not have made it to dinner.

I admired the late-model Mercedes Benz E-Class as I approached the car. Rocky got out and gave me a hug. I inhaled his masculine scent as my lips met his neck. He gave me a peck on the cheek before releasing me.

"Don't you dare. I got that," Rocky said as he opened my car door.

"Aren't we the gentleman?" I said as I stepped back while he held the door open. I sat down in the plush leather seats and checked my lipstick quickly as he got in.

"You look great, Fallon. Are you always this well put together?"

"Thank you. No, I'm not always this put together. But I wanted to get that response from you, and well, I guess this outfit works."

"It damn sure does. I hope you're hungry," Rocky said as he pulled off into the night.

Over dinner, we talked about our childhoods and upbringing. I knew there was something I connected to in Rocky. He happened to be part Indian—well, West Indian. His father is an Indian from Trinidad, and his mother is American Black. He's what they would call in Guyana a dougla, someone who is part Indian and black. That explained some of his fine features. His parents were still together like mine. He has no children. He almost became a father, but his ex had a miscarriage in her second trimester. He wants children in the future. We're the same age, and we both like to cook.

We laughed for hours over dinner, desert, and lots of wine. When we got to my door, as much as I wanted to invite him in, I stopped myself after he embraced me and left me with an intoxicating kiss that had my panties moist.

"Um, so I guess we'll have to do this again," I said after our lips separated, and the stars stopped fluttering around my head.

"Sooner rather than later, Fallon. I had a really good time talking to you tonight," Rocky said, looking into my eyes.

"Certainly. Well, I guess I better go in," I said, releasing myself from his warm embrace.

"Okay," Rocky said as he released me.

I put my key into the door, stepped inside, and closed the door behind me without looking back. I pressed my back against the door and threw a few air punches. *Damn it! Why didn't you let him in!* I thought to myself.

I kicked my shoes off and walked slowly through my dark large house. As I plopped down on my couch, it was at that moment that I wished that I'd asked him in. I was worried that if I slept with him on the first night, he may think the worst of me. Then I thought about it. *You're thirty plus. Do you really care what anyone thinks about the timeline of when you fuck? You are going to fuck him eventually anyway, aren't you? Whether it's tonight, a week, or a month from now.*

I got up and rushed to my front door hoping that I caught him before he pulled away. I opened my front door wildly, and he was standing there. I grabbed his face and planted a deep, wet kiss on him, holding both sides of his face. Rocky picked me up and carried me without breaking our kiss. He walked with me until he found a place to sit me. My kitchen was nearest to the entryway, so he placed me on my counter and stood in front of me in between my legs.

I opened my eyes and paused. The heat from between my thighs was radiating. It knew a dick was near, and it wanted him. At that moment, it had to have him, and so did I. Rocky stared into my eyes just as he had when he met me earlier that day, just as he had over dinner. I ripped his shirt open as buttons went in opposite directions, making noises as they hit my countertop and tile. I ran my hands over his pecs, and he took my bottom lip between his teeth and nibbled lightly. Rocky ran his hands up my thighs as he went from kissing me to using his tongue to massage my neck. I opened my legs wider, inviting him in as I closed them around his waist. Rocky carried me like this, with my legs wrapped around his waist, to my living room and lay me down on my cream, plush sofa. He stood over me and took what was left of his shirt off. I sat up on my elbows as he got on top of me, melting me back into the fold of my couch. Our clothed bodies meshed together as he pushed his groin into mine. I spread my legs wider eager to feel the real thing.

With a mouthful of my right titty, Rocky's tongue played with my nipple until I could hardly stand it. His nipple play was sending electric shockwaves straight to my clit, causing it to pulsate. When Rock moved his hand up my skirt and moved my panties to the side, I didn't protest. The wetness that he found when his finger rubbed my engorged mound of flesh told him that he was on the right track. As soon as his fingers met my moisture, he moaned. His finding of my fluid was a mutual pleasure.

Rocky let up on my erect nipple as he made a trail on my stomach with his tongue. I lifted my ass as he pulled my skirt and panties off in one swoop. Once they were off, I threw my right leg up so that it was perched near the top of my sofa. I was trimmed nearly bare, and as Rocky smiled my pussy smiled back at him. Rocky dove in and licked from the crevice of my ass all the way up my slit until his tongue hit the mound of flesh it was looking for. He applied the pressure that my body craved. The pleasure was so intense that my back arched as I held onto his head to steady the shivering waves that were taking over me. I ran my fingers through his curls, cursing under my breath and thanking God simultaneously for the bliss that my body was experiencing. As I erupted, Rocky applied force, holding my arms down as I tried to wiggle away. I wanted to free my clit from his mouth. The multiple orgasms were causing my heart to race, and the nerve endings of my vagina couldn't take anymore.

When he was satisfied that I was satisfied, he released my arms and sat down next to me, draping my legs over his.

"How do you feel?" he asked in almost a whisper.

I was still panting. "I feel great. Better than I have in a long time. Can't you tell?"

Rocky smirked. He knew that he had just blown my mind. We sat there quiet for a few moments lost in our own thoughts before I decided to break the silence.

"I hope you don't think poorly of me."

"What? Why would you say that?" Rocky's face scrunched up.

"Well, I met you all of this morning, and now, here you are, making me cum." I chuckled nervously.

"Baby. Baby, you're a grown woman. I'm a grown man. Would it have made you feel better if we had five more dates before we got here?" Rocky asked as he massaged my feet.

"I guess not. I don't know. You know some men judge women based off that kind of stuff, and then they don't take them seriously," I said.

"I don't play games, and I don't judge anyone. I been through too much and seen too much, trust me. I judge no one. I will say that I wanted you from the moment you stepped off that elevator this morning. So I'm glad to be here now, massaging your pretty ass feet." Rocky smiled.

I blushed. He had no idea that my feet were one of my erogenous zones. I licked my lips at the thought of getting filled up with the bulge I felt under my legs in his lap. I got up and straddled him, sticking my tongue deep in his mouth, tasting my own essence. He nearly swallowed my tongue as he ran his fingers through my hair.

This time, I took control, unbuckling his belt and unzipping his pants. Before I could grab at the waist, Rocky stuck his hand in his pocket and retrieved the square, gold wrapper. He stood up and took his pants off and sat back down. I took my place back in his lap and placed kisses all over his face as he took light nibbles on my neck. I could feel the heat from the log that sat between his legs pressing against my opening as my juices dripped on it, causing it to be covered in me as I grinded against it. It was feeling too good. I knew I needed to stop and open the Magnum before I just put him inside of me. I took the condom out of his hand and took this as my opportunity to get a good view of what he was working with. I tore the foil and placed it on the tip of his rock-hard dick. The head was beautiful, wide, brown, and large like a mushroom. I was tempted to put him down my throat, but I was too eager to have him fill me up. I began to roll the rubber over his shaft, enjoying the feel of his girth—nice and thick, just how I liked them. His length was long enough to hit every spot I needed touched.

When I reached the base, I sat back on his lap and lifted myself so that I could guide him in. I took a deep breath as he spread my opening to match his width. Rocky held onto my waist and guided me down until my canal covered his dick in its entirety. I exhaled and threw my head back. I had been waiting for this feeling. I began a slow, rhythmic grind, moving up and down, swirling my hips, and working his dick over. One hand held my waist and the other an ass cheek as I picked up speed like a jockey finishing a race.

Rocky panted and grunted. His mouth tight as he tried to hold back the explosion that was building and threatening to erupt. In one quick move, Rocky got up with his loins still inside of me and lay me back on the couch in the position I was in just a few minutes earlier. This time, instead of his tongue being in me, it was his dick. He showed me no mercy as he plunged deep in me shifting my walls.

"Uhhh oooh!" I let out a scream.

"Take this dick. It's what you wanted right?" Rocky said through deep breaths.

"Yessss… yeah… Ooohh, baby! Oohhh!" I cooed.

"This feels so fucking good. Shit!" Rocky bellowed.

Rocky's dick was like a shovel digging deep, removing any blockages, and clearing my drain.

His pumps became quicker as he kissed me deep. He whispered, "I'm about to cummm."

"Then cum, baby," I said as I pumped my pelvis and squeezed my vagina tight with around his massive tool what I had left.

Rocky moved out of me and pulled the rubber off and erupted like a volcano all over my stomach. "Arrggh! Damn!" he yelled.

Damn is right. I hope he didn't get none of that shit on my couch, I thought as I smirked. *We better hit the bedroom next time. This dude's a sprayer.*

A month later, I was sitting in the backyard of Rocky's garden-floor apartment, waiting for him to come out of the shower before we left out for the evening. I heard my phone buzz, and when I looked at the message, I saw it was from Keith. I started to not open it and just delete it without reading it, but I decided to see what the cheating asshole wanted.

Fallon, I haven't stopped thinking about you since you came into the station. Have dinner with me. Please. -Keith.

I didn't realize Rocky was out of the shower until I felt a drip on my shoulder. I looked up to find Rocky standing over me. His curls were dripping wet.

"So Keith finally got the nerve to text you, huh?" Rocky said as he made his way back into his apartment. Suddenly, I felt nervous. I didn't want Rocky to think I was entertaining the thought. I rushed in behind him. Looking at his well-built back covered with beads of water made me wet. The sight of the contrast of the white towel against his ebony skin wrapped tightly around his waist turned me on even more. He had his back turned to me when he spoke.

"Get your ass on the bed. Now!" he demanded.

I guess I was a little shocked. I didn't move.

"Did I stutter? On the bed, without your clothes. On your knees. Now." This time, he turned and looked at me with the sexiest, nasty look in his eye. He had the look of someone not here to play.

I quickly removed my clothes and complied with his orders. On all fours, I arched my back with my legs wide so that my opening would be exposed, and so I could brace myself.

The first slap came so unexpectedly that I jumped. Startled from the sting, I turned around and held my cheek. Rocky moved my hand roughly and pushed me back into position.

"You want to entertain other mothafuckas, do you?" Rocky said through gritted teeth.

The other cheek stung as he unleashed another whipping slap across my ass. I jumped, but I held my position. My opening was seeping fluids.

"You've made me work up a sweat, and now I'm thirsty!" Rocky commanded.

I moaned as I felt his mouth on me, drinking up and licking every drop he could from my pouring fountain. When his tongue reached my ass's opening, I quivered.

"Don't you dare move," Rocky said as he held my waist steady with his hand and darted his tongue in and out of my ass.

"Ooooh!" I whimpered.

"Turn around!" Rocky commanded.

I was turned around on the bed, still on my hands and knees and was met head-to-head with his dick.

I looked at it. A drop of precum was sitting at the tip, waiting for me to remove it with my tongue. Before Rocky could say another word, shout another command, or release another slap, I took it in and placed slow, wet strokes with my mouth and throat. Ensuring that his entire shaft was coated with my warm saliva, I relaxed my throat muscles and took him in. I gagged slightly.

Slap! I felt the sting on my cheek.

"What I told you about that? No gagging. Take this dick like I know you can." He scolded.

Rocky ran his hands through my hair, and as the head got him on the brink of explosion, he patted my head like I was his favorite pet.

"Yeah suck that shit," Rocky grumbled.

I took one hand and massaged his balls, which were drawn close to his body—my cue that he was about to release.

Rocky pulled himself out of my mouth and turned me around again. I started to crawl toward the head of his king-sized bed when he pulled me back by my ankles.

"Where you think you going? You ain't getting off that easy," he said as he dragged me backward toward him.

I assumed the position as he placed himself in me and grunted.

I was so wet that my body made gushing noises as he moved in and out of me. Rocky grabbed a fistful of my hair and pushed himself as deep as could. I could feel my ass cheeks pushed up against his taut stomach.

"You like this?" he asked as he pounded away.

"Yes. I love it. Please don't stop," I whimpered.

"Then show me," he said as he pounded harder.

Rocky reached around and took no mercy on me. He played with my mound of flesh and rubbed it just the way he knew I liked it. I pushed back on his dick, picking up speed as my orgasm threatened to be free.

Every muscle in my body tensed as I shook uncontrollably, releasing myself all over his shaft and balls. Rocky feeling the grip of my canal on him caused him to lose it as he spurted the contents of his sack inside of me. The strength he showed earlier was now nonexistent. He leaned into, me placing kisses on my damp back. We both gasped, exhausted as we climbed sticky and moist into his bed, forgetting about the plans we made for the evening.

######

As I drove to Summer's place, I thought about how the past three months had been like paradise with Rocky. Like we were made for each other. Who would've known that I would run into a man who knows how to give it as rough as I like to take it without thinking I'm crazy? I had a thing for a little violence in the bedroom. A little slap here, and a little paddling there. Perhaps a butt plug, a mask, or a little nipple pinching. No harm, no foul, just good lovemaking. Keith was good in bed, but he wasn't rough. There hadn't been many who knew what I needed without me having to direct them like a drill sergeant.

I knocked on Summer's door, and when she opened it, I realized that I had been so preoccupied that I hadn't seen my sisters in a minute. Summer and I embraced before we spoke.

"Girlie!" Summer exclaimed as she rocked me side to side. I pulled back from her to get a look.

"Look at you! I see you're over your Amber Rose phase, and you're letting your gorgeous locks grow out!" I said as I stepped into her place.

"Yeah, sis. I wasn't feeling it after a while. You really have to keep up on haircuts, and it starts growing as soon as you get a fresh cut. Who has time for that? I have some wine in the kitchen. Help yourself."

"As I should!" I said as I made my way to the kitchen to peruse her selection of wines.

I pulled out a fruity white, something light, and poured us each a glass. I made my way to her balcony where she was waiting.

"So what's been going on, lil' sis? You're glowing," I said as soon as I sat down.

"Look who's talking! You're glowing!" Summer teased.

"True, but you first," I insisted.

"Well, you already know Dre and I rekindled our relationship. He said he wanted to take it slow at first. You know, get to know each other all over again this time. I was with it. Plus, it was a good suggestion since I had to end things with Tori. Then Dre started coming down here. Like every weekend he's flying in. So things have been moving faster than I anticipated. I'm so in love with him, Fallon. So in love. I don't want to mess this up," Summer explained.

"You've learned from your mistake. There's nowhere to go but up in your relationship with him. I'm so happy for you both. When I met him at Spree's BBQ, I could see how much he adores you. How he looks at you when you speak. The way he holds the small of your back when he's next to you. It's what we all want—a man that hangs on our every word… a man that looks into our eyes and sees his future."

"You seem to have that with Rocky. I see you looking like everythang! How's Brianna doing in school?" she asked.

"Bri's doing great. She's going to split her time during the winter break between her father and I so she can spend time with her younger siblings. Rocky is good! Almost too good to be true. Who would've thought I would meet the man of my dreams through who I thought was the man of my dreams? Funny shit, wouldn't you say?" I said as I sipped my wine, thinking of the coincidence.

"I would say it was destiny. Keith didn't appreciate what he had with you, so it's his loss. You loved him something awful, but he couldn't keep his dick in his pants. So fuck his ass," Summer said as she threw up the peace sign.

"True indeed. Sometimes, I can't help but wonder how life would've been if Keith and I had made it. As much as I thought I was done with having kids, I would've given Keith one."

"Well, see how things work out with Rocky and perhaps give him one. Stop thinking about what could've been, and think of what could be. If you get stuck in the past, you will never get to make moves toward your future," Summer said as she clinked my wine glass with hers in a mock cheer.

"You know, Summer, for the baby of the crew, you sure give some good advice."

Summer turned down her mouth in an exaggerated way. "I'm younger than y'all, but baby girl has lived…"

I winked at Summer, knowing she had been through some experiences in her short life. We finished our small talk and gushed about the upcoming events. Summer gave me the inside scoop on some celebrity gossip she was about to have posted on her blog, and we chopped it up about that before I made my way home for the evening.

I finally had the house to myself again after a quick visit with Brianna. She decided she wanted to be in Cali for Christmas with her father and his little family. Yes, I said it… little family. Rocky and Brianna seemed to hit it off well, and I was none too happy. Rocky had been spending a ton of time at my place, often not going home after lovemaking and staying to make me breakfast. It was something that I could get used to, just not yet. I had come to enjoy my space. The solitude gave me the mental space to be creative. Perhaps I had gotten too used to the peace that being a single woman brought. With Rocky off to visit his family in New Jersey, I was looking forward to binge-watching Netflix and binge-eating ice cream. Besides, I had been putting in lots of time marketing my new line of scents, and any extra energy I had in reserve was long used up and gone. I had been feeling wiped out… like I needed to sleep for two days straight to get back to myself.

I lit my fireplace and prepared a bath in my Jacuzzi. I turned on Pandora to the Maxwell station and swooned, dancing with myself in my floor-to-ceiling mirror. After lighting a few candles and pouring in a little lavender oil, I sunk myself in. Resting my head back, I took in the scent and breathed deeply. The last few months had been a tornado of emotions, and I had been caught up in its rapture.

After drying off and oiling up, I tied my satin, pink robe tight around my waist and made my way to my living room to relax for the evening. My fireplace had the room nice and cozy. I couldn't wait to watch TV until the TV watched me. I had just picked up the remote and clicked the Netflix button when I heard my doorbell ring. *I'm not expecting anyone,* I thought to myself.

I started to just let whomever was out there stand there since I don't do drop bys, but I decided to answer it just in case it was important.

I could see a tall figure through the stained glass of my door. I peeked through the side panel and was shocked. I stood still for a moment as he rang the bell again. I know he saw me peeking through the side panel curtain.

I opened the door slightly. "What are you doing here?" The sight of Keith caused my heart to flutter a bit. There he stood, fine as ever, in a navy peacoat and jeans. His cap was pulled down over his bald head. It was chilly for an Atlanta night.

"I'm here to see you. Can I come in?" Keith responded.

I knew I shouldn't have, but I stepped back and opened the door wide, and he didn't waste a second stepping in.

"I know I should've called, but I didn't want you to have a chance to say no. Plus, I know your so-called man is on vacation, so I figured why not just stop by." Keith was arrogant.

"You should know if anybody, I don't do pop ups. I started not to answer the door. What do you want, Keith?" I folded my arms across my chest, suddenly realizing that I didn't have on much clothes.

"You smell good." Keith lowered his eyes.

"What do you want?" I avoided his gaze and started making my way to my living room.

"I want you. I want what we had. I know I fucked up. But you know it wasn't ever a case of me not loving you. It was just a case of me fucking because I could. You know there's a big difference between sex and love don't you?" Keith held my shoulders.

I shrugged away from his touch.

"Keith, we've been over for damn near a year. I'm happy now, and here you come. This may have worked six months ago when I was still pining over you. Missing you. Wanting you. But those days have come and gone. So if you don't mind, I was just about to enjoy some me time. Please see yourself out." I pointed toward my door.

"You think he can make you happy? He's just something for you to do right now. Someone to wet your kitty and lap up your milk. He's not the one, Fallon."

"And you are? Ha!" I laughed out loud.

"You know the answer to that, or you wouldn't have let me in. Admit it, you miss me as much as I miss you. Tell me you don't."

"I don't." I said with a straight face.

Before I could say another word, Keith was in my space, and his pillow-soft lips were on mine. I didn't stop him. I opened my mouth and allowed his tongue to explore mine. The hint of mint on his tongue was so familiar. I had craved his taste many nights. Keith slid his hand over my breast and down to the opening in my little robe. When he felt the flesh of my thigh. It didn't take him but a second to slide his hand up to the warm, moist mound between my thighs. I moaned at his touch. Keith untied my robe and lay me down on the furry, cream, white bearskin rug in front of my fireplace. He took turns sucking on my breasts. The warm air from his breath was welcomed on my nipples that had become erect as soon as they were exposed and the cool air hit them. I was writhing in pleasure under the weight of Keith as he began making his way down to my midsection. I opened my eyes and looked toward my couch and froze. Images of the first time I made love to Rocky flashed in my head. I saw my legs open wide on the couch with the man of my dreams.

"Stop!" I pushed his head.

Keith looked up confused. His eyes still full of lust.

"Stop. Let's stop. This isn't right," I said as I pulled my robe together, trying to hide what he had already seen so many times before.

"What do you mean this isn't right? Come on now. Stop playing." Keith leaned in to me, trying to finish what he started.

I got up and avoided his touch. "Please leave. I shouldn't have even let you in." I threw him his coat.

"You can't be serious. You're really asking me to leave? Fallon, what we have can't be duplicated. Trust me," Keith said snidely.

"You're absolutely right. I'm not trying to duplicate the bullshit! I think I've done a whole helluva lot better. Now get the fuck out," I demanded. I had enough of trying to coax him out.

Keith smirked. "I've been asked to leave better places. Take care."

I watched him sashay to the door all smug and shit.

I slammed the door behind him and ran to the shower and jumped in. *I messed up. I really just screwed up,* was all I could think to myself as I tried to wash any traces of him from my body.

I didn't realize that I hadn't touched my food until he said something. I had been craving homemade curry for weeks. I wanted it made just the way my mother cooked it with masala. But my nerves and the guilt that came with those things that you feel when you may have just lost the man you never knew you needed because you screwed up. I sat, moving the food around on my plate, taking turns stabbing at the potatoes. My stomach was queasy. I felt all kinds of mixed up—emotionally and physically.

"You've hardly touched your food. I prepared you this chicken curry and fresh roti, and you play over it," Rocky teased.

"I'm sorry, baby. I just have a lot on my mind." I didn't know what to say I couldn't make eye contact with him.

"Well, I'm all ears. Talk to me, baby, like I'm your therapist." Rocky chuckled.

"It's nothing. Tomorrow's another day, and I will feel better I'm sure."

"You know, Fallon, you've been a little weird since I got back. Is everything okay? With you? With us?" Rocky's tone was serious. He folded his arms across his body as he stood stiffly waiting for a good answer.

"I guess they are. Listen, I have to tell you something."

"What's up?" Rocky unfolded his arms and leaned in.

"Um… Well, while you were away, Keith stopped by." I took a step backward, waiting for his response. He seemed calm. At first.

"Okay, and… Wait, he stopped by? The fuck? You didn't let him in, did you?" Rocky's face contorted into an annoyed expression.

"I did. But—" I didn't get to finish my statement before he cut me off.

"But what, Fallon? But what? I know you not gone tell me you fucked him." Rocky got up from the table and began to pace.

"No! Not exactly." I began.

"Well, what?" Rocky seethed. I could see smoke coming from the top of his head.

"Listen, he kissed me, a-and I kissed him back. At first," I stuttered, putting my hand up like I was stopping imaginary traffic.

"You have got to be kidding me! After all I thought we had! What I thought we were building, and you let this busta come and fuck you?" Rocky was yelling.

"I didn't fuck him, Rock. I stopped it before it got that far. I knew it wasn't right, and I stopped it." Tears began to well in my eyes as I tried to explain.

"Yo, this is some wack ass shit you telling me. So what, I'm supposed to just go back to work knowing he's been with you? And I don't wanna hear that 'but he ain't fuck me' shit either. You played yourself, Fallon!" Rocky said as he grabbed his jacket and started for the door.

My heart was beating wildly, like horses stampeding. My head swooned. I felt dizzy. My stomach felt like it wanted to empty itself of its contents. I couldn't let him walk out of my house or my life. I grabbed for his arm, but with an aggressive shrug, he pushed my arm away.

"Rocky, please! You have to listen to me! I shouldn't have let him in, but you have to believe me… I stopped it before it went too far. I couldn't sleep with him when I thought about what I feel for you!" I stepped in front of him blocking the door, pleading my case.

"You're right. You shouldn't have let him in. Now get the hell out of my way. I'm not trying to hear none of the shit you kicking," Rocky demanded. The bass in his voice advised me to move out of his way before he moved me.

I again reached out and grabbed the back of his arm as he was heading out the door.

"Don't leave like this. Let's talk! Please," I pleaded.

Rocky kept walking and didn't turn around. When he jumped in his car and pulled off without looking at me, I knew I may have crossed the point of no return.

After the first week of texts that weren't responded to, I figured he was completely done with me. I thought about how I must've hurt him, hurt his feelings, and crushed his pride. Here he was, doing everything right, being everything I needed him to be, and that still wasn't enough for me to not allow Keith the time of day.

I had been feeling out of it for the past few days and decided that I would take myself to breakfast. I showered, and as I brushed my teeth my stomach began to move in waves. The bile from my empty stomach burned as it made its way past my esophagus and through my clenched teeth. I spewed the yellow all over my shower floor as I held my shower wall to steady myself. I felt weak as I used the showerhead to rinse my body of the traces of vomit and to clean my shower floor of the mess my empty stomach managed to give.

I stepped out of the shower and wrapped a towel around myself. I swiped over the fogged floor-length mirror and looked into my own eyes. I stretched my eyes wide at the person staring back at me. *This can't be happening.*

As I pulled my panties up I swiped my hand over the barely-there pouch that was forming on my lower stomach. I began to laugh out loud. I know I would've sounded crazy to anyone watching, but I couldn't help but think of the timing. I was pregnant. *How did I let this happen?* I knew better. I knew how not to have it happen, but acting like I did as a teenager got me in the same position I was in almost twenty years ago—pregnant and alone.

I pulled into Spree's driveway and sat parked as the tears rolled down my face. I pressed send on the phone. Spree answered after two rings. "What's up, boo?" Spree sang into the phone.

"I need to talk to you. Are you alone?" It was all I could say before the tears started to pour again.

"You wanna talk now or you want to meet up?" Concern resonated in Spree's voice.

"I'm in your driveway, sis. I need to talk now."

"Come on in. I'm opening the door now," Spree said as she disconnected the call.

I saw her door open as I got out of my car. Spree wrapped her arms around me and grabbed me in a full embrace. "Come on, girl. Let's go in. I have some tea on the stove."

We sat at her kitchen table wordless until she poured the tea and sat down across from me.

"What's wrong, Fallon? Did he do something to hurt you?" Spree leaned in with anger draped across her pretty face.

"No. I hurt him… by letting Keith come in, and I made out with him," I whispered.

"Okay. Well, men screw up all the time. He'll get over it, girl. Shit, he better get over it." Spree rolled her eyes.

"That's not the worst part. I don't think he's going to get over it."

"Then his loss. You can't be pining over no nigg—"

I cut her off. "I'm pregnant."

"Come again." Spree's eyes widened.

"I'm pregnant, and Rocky is not answering my texts. He doesn't want me anymore." I covered my face with my hands as if that would stop the tears from falling.

"Did you tell him you were pregnant? You took a pregnancy test?" Spree was full of questions.

"No I haven't told him, and I haven't taken a test yet. I know my body. Plus, my period calendar app says I'm twelve days late. I don't know why I didn't realize what was happening to my body. I should've known better! I haven't even known him that long. How am I going to go and get pregnant by some guy that I've been seeing for just a few months!"

Spree's eyes held sorrow for me, but I could also see a bit of sorrow for herself because her own fertility had been complicated.

"Well, you gotta take a test to be sure before you say anything to him. Let's run out to the store and pick one up. I'll even hold your hand as you piss in the cup," Spree teased in an attempt to make me laugh.

I laughed a little, even though tears streaked my face. "You better!"

"Welp, girlfriend, you's about to be a mammy, again!" Spree teased as she held up the test to my face.

"Shit! I knew it. I should've known with all that buckwild action we had going on that this would be the result. Damn! I'm so stupid! I don't know if I want to be a single mother yet again!" I huffed.

"Hush! Your mother helped you with Bri, and you got three sisters now to help you with this one, if you want to have it. Besides, weren't you saying that you wanted more kids just a few weeks ago?"

"That's when I thought the kids were coming with the man and the happily ever after!" I palmed my forehead.

Spree sighed. "You can still have your happily ever after, boo boo. The presence of a man doesn't dictate your happiness or your forever after. Believe that."

Spree listened to me whine and go on about the what ifs for the rest of the evening as she made me some homemade chicken soup, enough for a few days. As the moon shined and the stars glowed, I made my way back home to make a final attempt to reach out to Rocky. It was his baby. After all, he deserved to know.

The next morning, I picked up the phone and called Rocky, expecting to get his answering machine. I was surprised when he answered.

"Hey, Fallon." He sounded dry, but at least he answered.

"Hi, Rock. I'm surprised you answered the phone." I tried to sound upbeat.

"I was actually going to call you today sometime anyway. You have some things at my place, and I wanted to know if you wanted them."

"Yeah. Sure. Listen, Rocky I called you because I—" I didn't get to finish my thought.

"I'm leaving, Fallon. I resigned from the station last week. I can't work with him whether something happened or not. He's a snake, and I don't fuck with snakes."

It felt like all the air in my bedroom had been vacuumed out. I gasped. "Leaving? Leaving to go where?" I raised my voice.

"I got an offer in New York. WWPR-FM offered me a spot on their executive production team. I had dinner with the VP of programming when I was up there visiting my family a few weeks ago. It's a good opportunity. Plus, I'll be able to be closer to my family. There ain't nothing down here for me anyway." Rocky still sounded upset.

"I'm here." I hoped that he would reconsider what he just said.

"Yeah, you are, and that's just where I'm going to leave you."

I tried to hold them in. I wanted to scream "Fuck you! Go!" But the tears burned the edges of my eyes. "Rocky, I'm pregnant." I paused, waiting for a response, for a breath, for anything.

The phone was quiet for a few moments that felt like forever. I let out some air, relieved that I had gotten the words out, knowing I couldn't take them back.

"Pregnant?" The anger in his voice now subsiding.

"Yeah, pregnant, and before you even go there. I have not been with anyone but *you*!" I emphasized the you.

"Damn, Fallon. I should've known this was going to happen. We were so caught up in the mix, and I thought we were going to be together. Now what?" He sounded like he was talking to himself looking for an answer, not really waiting for my response.

"I don't know what to tell you, Rocky. I am going to have this baby, despite the fact that I don't want to be a single mother. I just hope you're able to be there for me and the baby in some way, shape, or form and that you don't let my mistake, which is minor in the scheme of things, stop us from moving forward."

Rocky cleared his throat. "I'm not sure what you consider minor, but breaking the trust in a relationship is in no way minor. A baby can only complicate things in a relationship that's already not working out. You should know this, Fallon."

"It is what it is, Rocky. I'm not trying to trap you. I'm self-sufficient, but you already know that, so I'm not telling you because I want anything from you. I just thought you should know." I pressed end on the call. I ain't never had to beg nobody for their company, for their attention, and I'm not going to start now. Rocky can kick rocks as far as I'm concerned. I threw my phone down on my bed and cried. I watched my phone's screen light up with Rocky's name, but I didn't answer it. He was being an asshole. Sure, I broke his trust. I knew it was wrong, but I also did the right thing in telling him how I had screwed up. That should count for something. *Shouldn't it?*

My doctor confirmed what First Response and my subtly-expanding waistline had already told me. I was pregnant. I had just stuck my key in the door when I heard his car pulling into my driveway. Rocky got out and grabbed a bag from the back seat. I ran my hand over my hair, making sure my slick back was still in place neatly.

"I just came by to drop off your stuff. I've been trying to get my place together before the moving company comes at the end of the month to ship everything." Rocky averted his eyes from mine. I could see him looking at my midsection.

"You been to the doctor yet?"

I placed my hand on my hip. I felt defiant and aggravated that he would ask anything about it since he was moving on. "Yes. I actually just came back from the gynecologist. Seems I'm a little over two months—about ten weeks according to her." I reached for my bag of items that he had resting on the strapped bag on his shoulder.

"Almost three months? Wow! Can you feel it?" Rocky said as he stepped back slightly to avoid me grabbing for the bag.

"Yep. Listen, I'll take the bag. Thanks." I held my arm out.

"No, I'll put it inside. You don't need to carry anything heavy."

I gave a sarcastic chuckle. "Well, by the look of things, I'll be carrying plenty of my own heavy bags over the next few months. So really, let me just have my shit so you can be on your way."

I unlocked my door and stepped in, ready to close it in his face. He held his hand out just as I was about to close it.

"Can I come in?"

I pulled the door back and stepped aside. My sense of smell had been intensified by being pregnant, and while the smell of colognes and perfumes on other people had caused me to feel nauseous, Rocky's scent was like an aphrodisiac. I inhaled deeply as he made his way past me. The lips below my waist became glossy with my love flow.

Rocky headed to the living room and sat down in the same place he did the first time we made love. "You know, Fallon. I love you. I loved everything about you. I thought we were tight for the small amount of time we were together. I didn't think you would be the one to play me so quickly for a dude that did you all types of dirty. That shit is crazy to me."

I sat down next to Rocky. Hoping he would give me the chance to explain without walking out again. I placed my hand on his thigh and looked him in the eye.

"I'm so sorry I hurt you. I don't know why I let him in. If I could go back to that night, I would've left him out there ringing the bell. I did not fuck him. I wouldn't do that. When you got back, I felt so bad. I had to tell you, even though I knew you may get as angry as you did and walk out. It was the chance I had to take because I didn't want any lies between us."

I took a deep breath before I continued. "I guess a part of me wanted to let Keith in just to turn him down. I wanted to show him how happy I was with you. How much he screwed up by letting me go. I had no business playing like that. In many ways, Keith's a weak spot. Not for my heart, but for my ego. How'd he cheat on me? I'm a great catch!" I laughed, hoping my joke would lighten the mood.

"I should've been enough for your ego, Fallon. Why did you need validation from Keith? Does he mean that much to you?" Rocky sounded defeated.

"No. Never as much as you mean to me." I hoped I sounded believable.

"When I saw you, I felt you were special and that our meeting was fate. Everything about you was what I always wanted in a woman. Your family's great, and your daughter's a beautiful product of you. Then you messed with him."

I played with my fingers like a little school girl. My nerves were on edge.

"Now you're having my baby. I don't want to miss a thing with my baby or you." Rocky placed his hand over my hands to stop them from moving.

I was hoping I was hearing right. "Does this mean you're not going to leave?"

"I signed a contract with the station in New York. It's an opportunity that I can't pass on. What I'm saying is that I want to try and make things work with us. With our little family we created, but trust is something we're going to have to work on."

All of a sudden, I felt alone in this. My mind flashed back to a time of desperation when all I wanted was to have someone to share the precious moments of parenthood with. The first smile, giggles, crawls, and steps. The late-night feedings, the snotty noses, all of the highs and lows that go into parenting. Even though I had my parents, I didn't have a partner to share that experience with when I had my daughter, and I didn't want to do it alone. Not again.

"I can't have this baby, Rocky. I just can't. I did the single parent thing already, and I have no interest in doing it alone again!" My chest rose up and down as I breathed heavily at the thought.

Rocky grabbed me by both arms. "What do you mean you're not having it? You must be out your mind to look me in my face and say that crazy mess."

I looked in his eyes and saw an anger that I didn't know he could possess. He was angrier than he was when I told him about Keith stopping by. It didn't matter to me though. My mind was made up when he said he couldn't turn the job down in New York. He had made his choice, and now I had made mine.

"You're leaving to begin a new life. New York's a big, bright place. You expect me to just be here with your baby when you decide to make time to visit?" I shook myself free from his hold. I put a little distance between us before I continued just in case he got fool.

"Besides, do we even really know each other? What has it been, three months? I would be a fool to have a baby by a dude I barely know. I'm no young high-school girl who doesn't know better."

Rocky closed the space between us, getting so close to me that I could smell the hint of toothpaste still on his breath.

"No, you're not. A few minutes ago, you sounded like you were all for bringing our baby into this world. But because I have a job that I need, you're going to get rid of it? Ain't that some slick shit. I never looked at you as the type to try and hold a baby over a man's head. But here you are doing the unexpected." Rocky rubbed his goatee as if he were in deep thought.

"Just. Don't. Leave. Me," I said between pecks on his lips. I know I sounded desperate.

Rocky slipped his tongue in my mouth, and I melted into him. When I felt him gather my legs and lift me from the couch, I opened my eyes. I relaxed every muscle in my body, allowing his strength to carry me, to take over for however long I could have him for. Rocky carried me to my bedroom and lay me down gently on my plush bed. My back relished the cool, soft feeling of my white down comforter. Rocky lay down next to me and stared at me while playing in my hair before saying anything.

"You're so beautiful, Fallon. I want you. I want my baby. Is there really a little me in there?" Rocky moved his hand to my belly and rubbed in circles gently.

"Yep. A little you or me. But it's definitely in there. Growing and making me tired, taking all of my energy," I said.

I stopped Rocky's hands as they rubbed my belly. "I want this baby too. I just don't know if it's the smartest thing to do. We haven't taken the time to get to know each other. We haven't even been on a vacation together, and now I'm having a baby? It's not right. I love you, but I can't do it. Let's try this getting to know each other thing again. If it's meant to be, we can try to have a child a year or two from now."

Rocky lowered his head in defeat. When he looked up at me, I knew he was in agreeance with what I said. It only made sense. Why bring another person into this world with parents who were so unsure of everything? At that moment, I just needed him to touch me, to make me feel that he still wanted me.

As I looked into Rocky's eyes, I saw nothing but compassion, hurt, forgiveness, and joy. All those things emanated from the dark pool of his eyes. Rocky gently put his head on my small but rounding belly. He leaned in like he was listening, but then he began to place kisses on my belly. He started at the top of my stomach right under my breast and softly kissed his way down to the top of my panty line. When he reached my panties, he looked up at me and smiled devilishly. He grabbed my panties by each hip and slowly pulled them down.

"You thought you was getting away with all this good stuff?" Rocky asked playfully.

"You was trying to let all this good stuff go!" I said as I moved my neck in a mock attitude and teasing manner.

"Well, that's a wrap. This is mine... now and forever. All this!" Rocky said as he used his tongue and parted the lips below my waist.

"Spring passes, and one remembers one's innocence. Summer passes, and one remembers one's exuberance. Autumn passes, and one remembers one's reverence. Winter passes, and one remembers one's perseverance." -Yoko Ono

Part 2

Six Months Later...

Wynter

And just like that... what once was is no more. This time last year, I was single and always down to mingle, if you get my drift. So as I watched the top of his shiny bald head as he knelt on one knee in front of me at what was just supposed to be a dinner party for friends and family, I was incredulous. I guess my lack of response threw him off.

"Wynter, did you just hear me?" Khalil cleared his throat.

It was like everything was moving in slow motion. I watched a bead of perspiration form on his forehead and slowly drip down his face.

"Wyn, will you marry me?" Khalil chuckled nervously as he gripped my hand a little firmer than he had been just a few seconds ago. I was thankful for the squeeze as it brought me out of my trance.

Marry? Is he serious? I am the happiest I've been in as long as I can remember. But how long will that last? All of these ideas and theories ran through my head before I could muster up a response. The silence in the back room of our favorite restaurant was palpable.

"Yes..." It came out as a whisper. But really it was loud enough for him to hear.

"Yes? You said yes, baby?" Khalil sounded like he needed reassurance.

"Yes. Yes, I will marry you! I love me some you!" I said as I grabbed Khalil and placed a kiss on his delicious lips.

I could hear the roars, screams, and the sounds of breaths that had been held waiting for my answer being released. I looked down as he placed what looked like a platinum, three-carat, princess-cut solitaire on my left hand.

I pushed my hand up above my head and yelled, "Your girl's about to be married!" As my closest sister friends gathered around me, I couldn't help but cry tears of joy.

My mother whispered in my ear as she hugged me tight. "I prayed for this for you. I was always worried that you would let the sins of your father keep you from this kind of happiness."

She was right. What I had been feeling with Khalil over the past year wasn't something I'd ever experienced or ever thought I'd experience. You see, I was always taught that in love, you had to compromise. I was self-made and self-maintained, so I didn't have to compromise with anyone, and it was something Khalil never asked me to do. When things seemed to be getting serious, Khalil opened up a small office out of Atlanta so that he could practice a few days a week there so that we could spend as much time together as possible. He never asked me to give up anything.

I waited and waited for the moment when he would mess up and disappoint me, but to date, he never had. Things were so good that by month two, I blocked all of the boy toys that I had in rotation, including good dick Vic.

I watched as Summer approached me, arms wide in a pretty coral sundress.

"I can't even believe it. Miss I'm Never Getting Stuck In A Marriage. Miss No Man Will Ever Lock Me Down. Well, chick, look at you now! You's about to be married!" Summer faked a deep-southern accent.

I couldn't do anything but playfully roll my eyes, knowing she was right.

"I know right. I didn't see this in my future, but I can't let the likes of Khalil Jameson walk out of my life. He's everything I never thought a man could be. So far anyway."

Summer scooted me out of earshot so that our conversation would be private. I watched young Summer who had grown into quite the woman place her hand on her hips as she began to speak.

"Wynter, listen, I'm always taking your advice. You seem to know just about everything. You're extremely beautiful but just as much an intellectual. But you need to stop being so skeptical. Stop with the so far, just stop." Summer placed her hand up before she continued.

"Enjoy everything you have waiting for you. Enjoy living in the moment. If it ever doesn't work out, which I highly doubt, then it just doesn't. But stop thinking every man is good for nothing. "

Instinctively, I rolled my eyes, but then I thought about it for a moment. She was right. I spent so much time thinking of all the ways it couldn't work that I didn't give it a decent chance at working.

"I will keep that in mind, little sister. Thank you for being a true friend who has become a family member. I just love you so much," I said as I grabbed ahold of Summer in a tight embrace. Since she restarted her romance with Dre, she had been glowing from the inside out. I missed seeing her, Spree, and Fallon as much as we used to, but we always managed to make a concerted effort to spend time together.

"There you two are! Everyone's looking for you! It's time for the toast!" Spree said as she entered the small crevice of space that Summer and I had managed to find for our little talk.

"We were just about to come back in there! Tell everyone to hold their horses. Including your little love crew." I joked.

"You know, Wyn, I think I've told you already, but I'm so damn happy for you," Spree said as she began to tear.

"Don't start, Spree-Spree! I can't bear to shed a tear. Besides, I refuse to lose my eye makeup behind y'all," I teased.

I grabbed Spree in a tight hug as we walked back to join the rest of the party. Spree had come a long way and finally seemed to be in a happy space. It took me a minute to get comfortable with her situation, but if she liked it, I loved it.

Later that night as I lay in bed watching Khalil's chest rise and fall, hearing the sounds of his light snores, I couldn't stop the fluttering of butterflies that raced through my belly. He had put in work after the proposal dinner, making my body shiver as if it was our first time. I held my hand up in the darkness, but the moon shined enough so that I could still admire the sparkling diamond that rested on my finger. I never ever thought I would be someone's wife, and I secretly felt a bit hypocritical for accepting his proposal after all the "trust no man" rhetoric I had been spewing since I could remember.

I tossed and turned, but the excitement of the day wouldn't allow my mind to rest enough to sleep. I had everything I didn't know I wanted. A booming career, I'm financially comfortable enough to take care of my mother, and now I have a man that couldn't be more molded out of my dreams in both my heart and my bed. I decided to get up and brush my teeth. It was a habit of mine to make sure my breath was fresh before he opened his eyes. I crept to the bathroom located in our bedroom, pausing at the doorway for a few seconds to watch him sleep. I smiled to myself and took a deep breath with the realization that this is really real.

Perhaps I'll even think about having a baby soon after the wedding, I thought to myself as I gave my mouth a final rinse I turned the light off and began taking light steps back to the king-sized bed purposeful in my desire not to wake my sleeping beauty.

The flashing light from the nightstand on his side of the bed caught my attention. There was no sound. The screen just lit up quickly and then dimmed. I started tiptoeing again, making my way to my side of the bed, hoping to get a few hours of shut eye before the sun rose. Just as I lay my head on the soft pillow, I saw the screen of his phone lighting up again from my peripheral vision. I was about to tap him just in case it was an urgent call from his daughters or their mom. I pulled the covers back and swung my legs over the side of the bed. *You're about to be his wife. See who's calling so you don't have to disturb him… if it's nothing.* That's how I made it make sense to myself that I was about to go pick up his phone and scan the missed call list.

I paused just as my hand reached the cool sides of the phone. *Maybe you should just wake him up.* I ignored my inner voice and recalled the pattern he used to get in his phone. I touched the screen and did the weird zigzag he had set up as his password. The screen illuminated in the darkness providing me with full access. Just as I was checking the missed call log, the square message box appeared, alerting me that a message had just come in. I swallowed the lump that had formed in my throat as my finger glided across the screen and navigated to the missed call.

"Two missed calls from Zara? Who the hell is that?" I mumbled out loud. I shifted the weight to my right leg as I took a stance, preparing myself to read the message that had just come in.

Zara: Seeing you last week was just what I needed. I didn't realize how much I missed you until I saw your face. Call me. Please.

A surge of heat ran from the bottom of my feet to the top of my head as soon as I read the last word in her text. Without thinking I slammed the phone down into his chest, causing him to spring up from his slumber.

"What the hell?" Khalil asked as his eyes widened at the sight of me standing there breathing hard while my hands were on my hips with my head cocked to the side.

"What the hell! No let me ask you this! Who the hell is Zara? Why is she texting you, and when did you see her?" I was yelling at the top of my lungs. I didn't care if my neighbors heard me.

"Baby, let me explain. It was nothing." Khalil put his hands up in front of him instinctively as if he knew the next blow would be something physical from me.

"You know what? You don't gotta explain shit. Get the fuck out!" I yelled as I quickly stomped across my room to the closet that I had let him hang a few pieces of clothes in. I began ripping his clothes from the closet, throwing them in his direction, not caring where they landed.

"Don't you think you're being ridiculous?" Khalil gave a nervous laugh.

I looked at Khalil. My eyes were squinted and burning as I tried to retain the tears that were at the brim of my eyelids.

"The only thing I was ridiculous about was thinking that I could trust you!" I pointed my finger in the direction of my bedroom door. "Now get the hell out! Please don't make me say it again!" I felt so defeated, so saddened, that my heart beat rapidly. I couldn't stop my hands from shaking.

I watched Khalil as he hurriedly threw on a pair of sweats and a T-shirt from the pile that sat nearest to him.

I trailed behind him as he made his way through my living room and to the front door. Just as he reached for the door handle, he turned to me. His eyes were low, all of the brightness the evening's joy had brought us dimmed.

"You're wrong, Wyn. If you give me a minute to explain, then I can clear this up, and we can go back to bed and back to doing us."

I shifted my weight to my right leg and crossed my arms. I must've looked crazy standing there in a bra and panties, but I wanted to look in his eyes when he answered. It dawned on me that I had heard the name Zara before. He mentioned her once when he talked about a past relationship, but he made it seem like it wasn't ever anything serious.

"Let me ask you two questions. Isn't Zara the chick you were dating before me?"

I tilted my head in his direction waiting for his response.

"Wynter," he uttered.

"Well?" I raised my voice an octave.

"Yeah, you know who she is." Khalil's voice was barely above a whisper.

I felt warm all over as I felt the heat raising up to the top of my head. I tried not to yell my next question, so I spoke through gritted teeth.

"Did you see her last week? Before you came here to see me? Or what?" Under my breath, I was saying a silent prayer that he was going to tell me that he hadn't seen her and that I was going to be able to look into his eyes and see that he was telling me the truth.

When I saw his head drop, I knew I wasn't going to hear what I wanted, but I was going to hear what I already knew.

"I saw her." Khalil didn't wait for me to respond. He opened the door and walked out. I slammed the door behind him and did something I didn't ever think I would do. I broke down behind a man. I needed the door for support as my back pressed against it, and the pain radiated from my stomach up. The tears that spilled from my eyes were those of disappointment. Not only disappointment in Khalil, but also anger at myself for getting involved so much that I forgot my own damn rules.

When my butt hit the floor, I felt some relief. The weight of everything could rest on my cool, wood floor. I pulled my knees to my chest and cried for what would never be.

Spree

It's odd. I had all of these plans for my life. What I thought it would be, especially once I got married—husband, dream home, a couple of children, perhaps a dog. I was on course, but then I wasn't.

The warmth from their bodies had been something I longed for every night, and it was strange when I woke without them. I breathed in deeply. The lavender oil that she used in her hair was always a welcomed pleasure on the mornings when I woke with her back against my breast and the curve of her ass against my pelvis. His mouth was on my shoulder, and his arm draped over me, landing on the edge of her arm. My ass was firmly planted against his morning wood with the warmth of his heartbeat against my back.

This was how I had been waking up nearly every morning for the past few months. Sometimes I'm in the middle, other times not, but this triad, this love triangle, had quickly become the most fabulous and exquisite romantic relationship I had ever experienced. Initially, things had been a kind of push and pull between Omari, Kris, and I, with Omari and I sneaking off for separate sexual excursions, only sometime including Kris. After a few times, it didn't feel right creeping around behind Kris's back. Besides, I found myself enjoying the taste of her. It was a taste I had come to crave just as much as I craved Omari's touch.

It was unconventional and something my loved ones had to get used to, but it's my life, and it's the lifestyle I chose. I had even begun having both Kris and Omari accompany me to family events and friend gathering functions. I could see the look of disdain and curiosity on people's faces as they tried to figure if Omari was with Kris or me or if Kris and I were in a relationship. We'd often shut people up when we would each take turns exchanging mouth-to-mouth kisses with each other. It really is something to see folks' eyes widen in astonishment, disgust, lust, and often jealousy.

After my divorce, I felt like I was kind of floating through life. I spent money getting myself in physical shape, but I had no idea what to do with myself. The settlement made it so that I got to keep my home—mortgage free of course—my cars, and enough money to give me the freedom to decide when I wanted to work or not, if ever. The awe, shock, and confusion about what I was doing with this three-way love affair got me to thinking. I had so many thoughts and emotions. For the first time in a long time I felt complete.

I decided I wanted to write a book to share my experiences in a polyamorous relationship. Trust me, if you had asked me a year ago if I could ever have seen myself involved in something like this, I would have laughed in your face and maybe challenged you to a fight. I never thought I could be attracted to a woman, let alone be attracted enough to want to keep my face buried in her snatch, and here I am, six months in and not looking back.

I decided on a tentative title for my book, *He, She, and Me*. It would be loosely based on my relationship, or perhaps I would make it a book of interviews with others in my situation. When I initially told Wynter, Summer, and Fallon, they each had their own thoughts about it. They even went as far as to call it "swinging". Apparently, they had no clue about what a polyamorous relationship was because it's certainly not swinging, even though there's nothing wrong with that either. My girls were so confused and wondered how I could share Omari. How I could share his love, affections, and man meat. I tried to explain, but they just didn't seem to get it. So I think a book may be a great way to get out all of the pleasures that this situation has brought, and they're not just physical.

The continuous sound of my phone buzzing disturbed my comfortable space and my train of thought as I peeled myself from in between my two sleeping lovers to retrieve it. I hated to leave my warm position, but my phone's constant buzzing meant I was receiving multiple text messages, and from the sound of things, they were coming in at a rapid pace. I unlocked my phone and began reading. I covered my mouth so that the gasp that threatened to escape my mouth would stay in. Naked, I threw on my satin kimono-style robe and made my way out of my bedroom. I couldn't take my eyes off of my phone's screen.

I could hear Wynter's pain through her messages, each one sounding more desperate and hurt than the next. She explained that she saw a late-night text from Khalil's ex-girlfriend and that he had apparently been seeing her behind Wynter's back. I couldn't believe it. Khalil. Suave, mature, dream guy, and gentleman were all the words I associated with him. I sat at the bar in my kitchen reading Spree and Summer's responses before I could type my own.

What does one say when your best friend's heart has just been broken? I did something I hadn't done in years, nervously I bit my nails, careful of my response. This wasn't just any old situation where a guy cheats on his girl. This is Wynter, who had a hard-enough time even trusting a man to date him exclusively to Wynter the independent inviting him space into her home to meeting his family to Wynter, whose motto was *I don't trust a single one of them fuckers*, accepting his proposal for marriage just the evening prior.

"Guess it's better she found out now," I mumbled to myself as I stared at my phone screen. My hands shook slightly as I gripped the phone and began to swipe.

Me: *Wyn, I'm coming over. Be there in less than thirty.*

There was nothing else for me to say or do. I had to be there to hold her hand through her tears just like she had been for me years earlier when she stepped out of her attorney role and held me as I cried with uncertainty about my life without my man.

I ran back upstairs and looked at my lovers. They had moved close since I vacated my spot in the middle, craving the body heat that our bodies created. I pulled out a sweat suit, took a whore's bath, just wiping down my lady parts, brushed my teeth, and started for the door.

Just before I left my bedroom, I paused and turned to look at the pair, snuggled in the way they did when it was just them two. Everything in me wanted to peel out of my clothes and crawl back to that safe, warm place between them. Instead, I jogged down the stairs and out the door. I had to be there to get my girl through this phase in life. This pain. Just as I started my car, the screen in the car notified me that I had a text message coming in from Khalil. I pressed the screen to open the message as I backed out of my driveway.

Khalil: *It's not what she thinks. Can you talk?*

Summer

I stepped into the dimly-lit parlor and scanned the room. My oversized shades and large, black, wide-brim hat were made for days like this. I smoothed down my form-fitting black Badgley Mischka sheath dress, always feeling the need to be impeccably dressed. I could feel the grip Dre had on my hand tighten as faces turned back toward us.

"It's going to be alright baby," Dre whispered in my ear as we slowly made our way down the narrow path in the small chapel that was packed to capacity. The past twenty-four hours had been an emotional roller coaster. From getting word just a few days prior that a funeral was being held for my father in New York to my best friend getting engaged to the love of her life, all to receive a text message as I'm boarding a red-eye flight saying the engagement and relationship was over.

We had literally flown in from Atlanta right after attending Wynter's surprise engagement dinner party. Early that morning, I received a message from my brother Kareem, asking if he would see me at our father's funeral, and although I had booked a ticket to New York so that I could be there, I was having mixed feelings about if I had a right to go. Despite the fact that I hadn't seen or spoken to the man I called Daddy for almost a decade, I was devastated nonetheless. The years that I had him in my life were good years, but when he and my mother's marriage fell apart, he didn't want shit to do with me. Treated me like I never existed, and for that, I considered not going to his homegoing; however, seeing as I turned out better than they would've expected, I decided to show up to my old neighborhood and show out and let them see that the little bastard they left for dead didn't die. Instead, I flourished.

I wanted to cry and scream out of frustration for all the years I felt disowned when I saw my brother Kareem approaching me. He gave Dre a once-over and nodded a hello as he held his arms out and grabbed me in an embrace that I was reluctant to return. I felt a surge of anger soar through me as I pulled back and away from Kareem. Kareem could feel the cold aura that was seeping from my pores. *Don't come playing "big brother" now, negro. You didn't give a single fuck about me when you found out I wasn't your father's daughter. Your friend pimped me out and had me selling my ass,* I thought to myself as I turned my mouth down into a slight snarl at the sight of his tears.

With various sets of eyes watching me, I removed my shades and held Dre's hand as it became my turn to view my father's body. I looked down at the shiny, copper-colored coffin and thought it would be something he picked out for himself. There was a point in my life where the sun rose and set in his eyes. I idolized him. He was my everything, and then I became his nothing. The pain and confusion that caused my young heart and mind had been irreparable. As I stood over him, his eyes closed tightly, he looked like he was asleep on the couch in our brownstone on a Saturday afternoon. He hadn't aged much. The cream-colored suit they had put on him complemented his dark complexion well. I shook my head as a tear escaped my eye. I didn't want to cry, but the more I fought the tears, the more they replenished and made more. Dre draped his arm around my shoulder and rubbed my back, letting me know he was there and was my support.

Dre ushered me into a pew that seemed to be reserved for family. It was directly behind where Kareem and what looked like his wife and children were seated as well as none other than my father's girlfriend, Debbie. Debbie wasn't only my father's girlfriend, but she was also my mother's best friend until she told my father that I wasn't his child. It was as if Debbie could feel me burning a hole in the back of her skinny ass neck. I was drying the remaining tears from my eyes as she turned around, and we made eye contact. Debbie's thin red lips were tight and turned down slightly, but what her mouth didn't say her eyes did. She commenced to rolling her eyes the way young girls did with a bit of a neck roll that let you know they had beef. In return, I smirked at Debbie as I dried my tears. I knew she couldn't stand me. As I think back, she never could. I winked at her before she turned around, knowing that would piss her off even more.

Quite a few people from the block and locals from the neighborhood approached me with kisses and condolences as we stood outside the sanctuary after the service. Dre asked me if I wanted to go to the burial, but I had paid my respects and was ready to close that chapter and move on. Dre had to park a block away, and while I was waiting on him to pull his late-model Mercedes Benz up to pick me up, Kareem approached me with his family.

"Look at little Summer looking all glamorous and fancy. You look like the princess we always thought you were," Kareem teased. He pointed to the pretty blonde standing next to him.

"This is my wife, Karen, and these are my daughters, Missy and Jazz," Kareem said proudly as he pulled the curly, sandy-brown-haired little girls in front of me.

"Hello, pretty girls. It's very nice to meet you. I'm your aunt Summer."

Both of the little girls, who looked to be no more than ten, giggled the way little girls do when a stranger compliments them.

"Where's Rich? I'm surprised he missed Dad's service," I mentioned.

"Yeah, me too. He has mom living with him in Texas where he's stationed. I don't think he kept in touch with Daddy like that. Debbie was funny style. She made it hard for everyone," Kareem said.

"Don't I know it," I said as I looked away in search of Dre's car. I was hoping to end my conversation with my brother.

Just then, I saw Dre pull up. "Well, it was good seeing you, brother. You have a beautiful family. Take care of them," I said as I started to walk away.

Dre was holding the passenger door open for me, and just as I was about to get in, I saw Kareem jogging over to me.

"Summer! Before you go wherever it is that you go, I thought you should know that Daddy left the brownstone to you. It's nearly paid off from what I hear. The formal reading of his will is tomorrow at noon, but I just wanted to give you the heads up."

"What? Why would he leave me the brownstone?" I was astonished.

"Only he can answer that, Summer. It was something that he wanted to do I guess. You know Debbie's not happy about that," my brother teased.

"I won't be around tomorrow, but text me the information for the attorney who's handling his estate, and I'll be in touch," I said as I sat in the car.

As Dre and I pulled off, I wondered why after abandoning me he would turn around and leave me the one thing that had any monetary value in his life. I smiled inside, thinking of the joy I would have when I got to tell Debbie that I wanted her out immediately, or I would be forced to physically remove her, which I had no problem doing either. She was still owed the ass whooping I couldn't give her as a child.

Dre interrupted my thoughts as we drove across the Brooklyn Bridge on our way back uptown to his place.

"Are you okay? I know today's been a lot for you," Dre said solemnly.

"I'm okay. Today was like closure for me, baby. Well, at least somewhat. At one point, I thought I would be able to speak to my father and ask him why he didn't want me. Why after treating me like I was his favorite person in the world he could turn on me so easily. I was a kid, innocent to the adult drama he had with my mama, and he threw me to the wolves. I know I wasn't his biologically, but he was the only father I ever knew. That had to count for something. Don't you think?"

"I don't know, baby. Maybe him giving you the house is his way of apologizing. After he got over whatever he was feeling, he probably came to his senses and realized that none of what happened with your mom and him was your fault. Sometimes people realize their mistakes when it's too late."

"That's so true. That's why I'm so thankful that you gave us another shot," I said.

Outside of my sister-friends Wynter, Spree, and Fallon, Dre was all the family I had. He really was the love of my life.

"You know, Summer, I've been thinking," Dre said as he rubbed my thigh with his free hand.

"I like when you think. What've you been thinking about?" I asked, hoping his thinking included me with my legs wrapped around his neck.

"Well, we've been putting in a lot of miles across the sky. Not that I mind, but I wanted to ask you to formally move in with me. I know you have your office in Atlanta, but you can blog from here. We can set you up with some office space in Soho or wherever you want. You know downtown BK is booming too," Dre offered.

I didn't respond for a few moments. I had been spending a lot of time in New York anyway, and as much as I liked Atlanta, I hadn't ever really planned on making it my permanent home.

"What can I say but yes? I want to be with you every minute of every day, Dre. SkyMiles are nice, but I'm starting to feel like a nomad at this point." I joked.

"Then it's settled. Life's so short, Summer. I need you. Don't disappear on me again," Dre said as he picked up my hand and kissed it.

"Speaking of SkyMiles... you know I'm scheduled out first thing in the morning. I have that interview scheduled with you know who. She's giving me the exclusive on that television producer of the reality show who's supposedly on the DL. This is an exclusive, and I can't miss it," I said.

"I know, baby. I know. Let me get you upstairs and out of that dress so I can give you something to think about while you're up in the air," Dre said sexily.

######

I was staring out of the window of the commercial flight as it landed in the early-morning hours of a gloomy Atlanta. My mind was still musing over the orgasmic blast I had a few hours earlier granted by Dre. I closed my eyes and discreetly squeezed my legs together tightly, imagining that his tongue was back in its place. The thump and bumps, caused me to open my eyes as we hit the tarmac a little rougher than I liked. Since we had a few moments of idle time as we waited to deplane, I took my phone off of airplane mode. As soon as the electronic signal showing that I had service was displayed, my phone began to ding as if I had it turned off for days.

Looking at the first message from Dre saying that he missed me already made me blush. I expected a message from him to be the first one I saw. The next message that came in had me inpatient and eager to deplane the flight. It was from Fallon. She needed us. I was thankful to be in Atlanta when she needed me. I tossed my carry-on over my shoulder and walked at a rapid pace through people in the large airport. Luckily, I got a cab as shortly after I stepped outside.

The young, foreign cabbie turned around as I sat in the late model sedan.

"Where can I take you today?" he said his accent thick.

"Northside Hospital please," I said.

I sat back and pulled out my phone to text my assistant.

Me: Move my meeting to tomorrow. Something came up. I want the exclusive. Tell her I can do breakfast. Her choice. It's on me. And apologize for me.

The last few days had been hectic. Everything seemed to be happening all at once. I closed my eyes and took a deep breath and mumbled one of my favorite quotes out loud to myself, "For all that is happening now, there is a season for everything under the sun, even when we can't see the sun."

Fallon

I sat on the side of my bed trying to decide if the pressure I was feeling was really me having to empty my bladder again or not. I was so tired of getting up multiple times throughout the night to waddle to the bathroom, and when I'd finally get comfortable in bed again, so that I could try to get some sleep, I'd have to get right back up. So I sat there, looking at the bright numbers on my cable box as the numbers changed. Finally I got up and decided to give in to the pressure and go relieve myself.

As soon as I crossed the threshold into my bathroom, I felt a popping sensation and then the rush of water as it cascaded down my thighs and over what used to be my ankles. I had been having what they call Braxton-Hicks Contractions for the past month, and although I was less than two weeks away from my due date, I didn't think it was going to happen today. I grabbed a towel and dropped it on the floor to dry up the fluid. All the pressure I thought I was feeling to use the bathroom vanished, so I brushed my teeth and splashed some water on my face. As I dried my face, I looked in the mirror and admonished myself for the stupidity of all of this. *You knew what you were getting yourself into. Now look at you. In labor and alone.*

Before I got dressed, I texted Rocky and let them know that I was in labor and about to drive myself to the hospital. I messaged my daughter, my parents, and I texted my girls to let them know as well. Rocky and I had somehow salvaged our relationship with him making frequent visits to Atlanta at least twice a month. He had planned to fly in a few days ago but said he had to stay in New York because he had to be at the radio station that week because they had a mega star guest set to interview.

Rocky called me almost immediately with a nervous edge in his voice.

"Baby, are you okay? I'm coming. You know I have my open airline ticket. I'm on my way to JFK. I already had my bag ready." He rattled off without taking a breath.

"I'm okay. The contractions are waxing and waning, but I know what's coming, so don't expect this level of calm when you speak to me again," I said as my baby gave me a good kick in the side. I kept my conversation with Rocky short. Both of us was in a transitory state, trying to get from one place to another. I grabbed my Gucci weekender that had been packed and ready for the past two months with all of me and my baby's essentials and headed out the door.

I checked in at the beautifully-decorated labor and delivery unit of the hospital. Just as my doctor and nurse finished examining me, they let me know that I was about four centimeters dilated and had a ways to go. As they were exiting my room, in walked Wynter along with Spree. I looked at Wynter and saw the hurt she had been going through written all over her face, even though she smiled when her puffy eyes met mine.

They each planted kisses on my cheek and took their position on opposite sides of my hospital bed. Shortly after they arrived, my parents got there. My mother held my hand and reassured me that she would help me as much as she could. She and my father had been reassuring me of their support throughout my entire pregnancy, especially when I would second-guess my choice to keep the baby.

I watched the monitor that would relay that another contraction was coming just before the pain began. In between contractions, we laughed as they tried to distract me and my attention away from the fact that Rocky was not there.

It was as if the wind had blown her in. Summer appeared, rushing through the door like she was being chased. I had to chuckle at the sight of how flushed her cheeks were. She greeted my parents and the girls and gave me a peck as she rubbed my hair away from my forehead.

"We gone have to bun you up, girl!" she said as she ran her hand over my hair that had grown past my bra strap in length.

"Mom, can you text Bri and let her know I'm okay? She said she wanted to be kept in the loop with what's going on," I yelled out.

A few hours had passed, and my contractions had begun coming in faster and getting stronger. I was trying to hold off on getting an epidural, but the pain had become so excruciating that I thought the baby was going to tear me in half. Everyone took turns at my bedside, but as the pain increased, my patience decreased. I was becoming aggravated and irritated at the sight of them all. As thankful as I was for their presence, it hadn't gone unnoticed that my child's father was nowhere to be seen.

Dr. Cambria came in with the gray-haired anesthesiologist, making light-hearted jokes trying to get me to laugh through my pain. I was in agony and was happy to receive the epidural that would give me some relief. I had been in labor for close to eight hours, and as my contractions intensified, I knew that my baby was ready to make its way into the world. I looked at the weary faces of my loved ones who all seemed to be nervous and lost in their own thoughts throughout the day.

The doctor lifted the covering that draped over my legs and propped my legs in the stirrups to get a look at what my cervix was saying. The top of his head disappeared between my legs, and I felt the pressure from his hand as he felt around in me. He popped up and pulled the surgical mask down under his chin.

"Looks like you're about ready to start pushing, my dear. You're just about dilated to ten centimeters." Dr. Cambria started shooting off orders to the nurses, and they started moving around the room quickly. I was hoping my father would be back in the room before the baby came. He left to get some rest for a few hours and was going to be bringing food back for everyone else. It had been a long day.

My mother held my right hand as she had done twenty years before when I brought my daughter into the world. I began to tear as I reminisced that I was about to do this all again, and I really didn't feel much better emotionally about it then I had as an adolescent.

Wynter took hold of my left hand as I bore down and began to pant out breath between my efforts to get what felt like a bowling ball through a drain in a sink.

Exhaustion was setting in. There's certainly a marked difference in pregnancy when you're young compared to when you're in your thirties. I was emotionally underdeveloped at fourteen to give birth, but at almost thirty-five, I felt physically unprepared for the beating my body was taking. I closed my eyes and said a silent prayer that my body and baby would cooperate and relieve me of the agony I was in.

Just as I opened my eyes, Rocky came rushing in, prepped and ready in green hospital scrubs and a scrub hat on his head. I smiled. My strength seemed to return at the sight of his face. Wynter smiled and rubbed my hand before letting it go and giving her position at my side to my man. I could see the relief and happiness on the faces of my mother and my friends in the room.

"Boobie, I was trying to get here before our baby arrived. Thank you for holding on," he said as he leaned down and placed a kiss on my sweaty forehead.

"You're almost there superstar. Let's welcome this little one into this world. Now give me another push. Take a deep breath, and give me a nice strong push. Make it good, and you'll have your baby in your arms soon," Dr. Cambria said as he assumed the position in front of me like he was on the football field waiting to be passed the ball.

With my jaws clenched tight and my teeth gnashing, I bore down and squeezed Rocky's and my mom's hands tightly. I was determined to get this baby out with this push. I could hear random voices cheering me on as if I was in a race, but the only voice I focused on was my doctor's. I relied on his coaching to let me know if we were near the finish line or not even close. I felt a surge of relief, and then I heard it. My baby's little cry. All of the pain, nervousness, and anxiety I was feeling vanished after I heard the cry and the words from my doctor.

"It's a boy!"

Reason, season, or lifetime...

People come into your life for a reason, a season, or a lifetime. When you figure out which one it is, you will know what to do for each person.

When someone is in your life for a reason, it is usually to meet a need you have expressed.

They have come to assist you through a difficulty, to provide you with guidance and support, or to aid you physically, emotionally, or spiritually. They may seem like a Godsend, and they are. They are there for the reason you need them to be.

Then without any wrongdoing on your part or at an inconvenient time, this person will say or do something to bring the relationship to an end. Sometimes they die. Sometimes they walk away. Sometimes they act up and force you to take a stand. What we must realize is that our need has been met, our desire fulfilled; their work is done. The prayer you sent up has been answered, and now it is time to move on.

Some people come into your life for a season because your turn has come to share, grow, or learn. They bring you an experience of peace or make you laugh. They may teach you something you have never done. They usually give you an unbelievable amount of joy. Believe it. It is real. But only for a season.

Lifetime relationships teach you lifetime lessons, things you must build upon in order to have a solid emotional foundation. Your job is to accept the lesson, love the person, and put what you have learned to use in all other relationships and areas of your life. It is said that love is blind, but friendship is clairvoyant. –Unknown

Other Novels by Mahogany Star

Where Secrets Lie

Where Secrets Lie Pt. 2

Sex Degrees of Separation

Summers Heat

Follow me on Instagram@ MahoganyStar

www.ingramcontent.com/pod-product-compliance
Lightning Source LLC
Chambersburg PA
CBHW032136170626
46808CB00006B/2264